PEACETIME

Peacetime is Dedicated to:

My parents Maria Lidia and Ruben, and to Hilda, Marina, José Luis, Ruben, Bonnie, and all my munchkins.

᠋᠋᠋᠋ᔕ ᔕ ᔕ ᔕ

Thanks to Christina Herrera for believing in my book at its inception, more than ten years ago.

Thank you, Jim Vale. No one has been a better friend. You have defined the word friendship. I will never forget your support through my roller coaster life.

Thank you, Pete Duarte, Cesar Caballero, Arturo Lechuga, Rebecca Ramirez, Ben Rubio, and Debby and Clay Dugger for being amongst my most ardent supporters.

PEACETIME

Spirit of the Eagle

Elena Rodriguez

CHUSMA
HOUSE

CHUSMA HOUSE PUBLICATIONS

Published by Chusma House Publications
P.O. Box 467, San José, CA 95103-0467

ISBN: 0-9624536-9-2

Library of Congress Catalog Card Number: 97-7502

Cover Illustration/Production
Hiram Duran Alvarez

Edited by
T.W. Hullm

First Printing 1997

Patson's Press, Sunnyvale, California

Printed in Aztlán

Looking Back at Zero Week

Medrano's skin glistened as she did what seemed to be the hundredth pushup. She took in quick bursts of air since her lungs were not capable of taking deep ones. Salt water poured from her forehead onto her eyebrows. Tiny drops touched her eyes and made her vision blur. She had never sweated much before in her life.

"Damn, Damn," whispered a voice behind Medrano.

A small smile spread across her face. She recognized the voice. It was Peck's. Her swearing reminded Medrano that she was not the only one suffering. There were others who hated Army PT, physical training, as much as she did.

Her arms trembled as she attempted to do another pushup. She let out sounds like a whining dog. The thought, "no pain, no glory," resonated in her mind. It was something the drill sergeant had tried to drill into them, but the next thought that came to mind was, "bull-shit."

She detested male pushups. They were not the female kind where the knees were bent. These were the macho kind where the weight of the body was placed on the shoulders. Medrano could not think of a harsher pain than the one her shoulders was screaming out. It upset her that she was so physically weak and that she was nowhere close to doing "good" pushups where the body went up and down with rhythm and precision. As it stood, her stomach reached the ground before the rest of her body did, making her look awkward. Her limited strength would not allow her body to go up and down evenly or even to go low enough to touch the ground and then pull up again. Sergeant Acosta had taught them a neat trick—to straighten up their bodies while doing pushups. They were to tighten their behinds so their body would be rigid enough to stay straight. This would prevent their stomachs from crashing to the ground before the rest of their body knew what was happening.

Still, Medrano just could not get the hang of it.

"Double, double damn," Peck said.

Medrano, and the other females around Peck, stifled a laugh. They knew they would really be in trouble if the sergeant caught them laughing while they were in PT. The Army did not take such things lightly. A soldier was supposed to take anything concerned with the military seriously all the time. Laughter belonged to civilians.

It was not that long ago that she had been a civilian. It seemed centuries ago when, in fact, it was days. She could hardly remember when she slept late, dressed in anything other than green, or even laughed when she felt like it. This had all been B.A.—Before the Army. She tried to get her mind to go back to that happy time in order to concentrate on something other than her physical pain. However, her mind would only take her back as far as when she got on the plane to Fort Jackson.

It had been her first plane ride, and she had continually wrung her hands. When she changed flights in Georgia, she found many new recruits, male and female, going to the same destination. Their rowdiness caused her to wring her hands even more.

When they finally arrived at Fort Jackson, it was 10 p.m. A sergeant screamed at them to form two lines—this was her first clue as to what Army life would really be like. She thought about being in South Carolina now a place she had never been. It was green like a jungle and unlike the dry desert to which she was accustomed. That had been the first of many firsts for Medrano. She had never been without her family, she had never been in a fort, and she had never been screamed at like that.

The new recruits were put on a bus and immediately taken to Fort Jackson. The once gregarious group on the airplane was quiet on the bus since the sergeant eyed them with a look that would stop drug dealers from dealing.

Thoughts were spinning in Medrano's head. Already she was millions of miles away from home in her mind. Already her thought patterns were moving to a new way of life. Gone was her freedom. Gone was her sleep. Gone were her friends. Gone were her jeans. Gone was her first name, Eliza. Gone was high school.

She was doing something her peers thought was crazy since she had received a scholarship to go to college. What they didn't know was that the scholarship and government grant wouldn't begin to cover all her expenses. She could have gotten a job, but her grades would have suffered. The Army seemed the best choice considering the Army College Fund. Besides, she was sick of her parent's house which seemed to be falling apart every time she turned around. Now she'd be able to help them fix it.

Ever since she could remember, her family never lived in a comfortable house. The air conditioners and heaters were either nonexistent or malfunctioning; the few rooms were too small; and the walls were ugly no matter how much bright paint was heaped on

3

them. Yet, her parents could barely afford the shacks they lived in, so she would comfort herself with the fact that at least they were not homeless.

Unlike herself, most of the other top students lived in beautiful homes, led middle class lives, and had parents with careers which allowed them to pay their children's college education. She always felt different from them, so in school she was reserved and fantasized about having an exciting life. She did not want just a comfortable life. She wanted something out of the ordinary.

Medrano remembered the first time her brother Teodoro, who was eight years older, had come back from serving in Europe. He looked so important and handsome in his green uniform, Medrano had thought. His face was lit up with the mystique of travel, of being in foreign lands and places. Teodoro bought an old camera and filmed his exploits in Europe. Eliza sat in the dark watching home movies with her mouth wide open and pretending she was on the train in Spain, hanging out in the Eiffel Tower, or floating by castles. It had seemed natural when she had gone to the recruiter's office and enlisted.

"Have any kids?" The recruiter had asked her when he was filling out the forms.

"No," answered a nervous Medrano. Second thoughts thumped in her brain. She kept trying to focus on the brochure on his desk which said, "Army. Be all you can be."

"No kids at all?" His eyes showed surprise.

"No. Is the Army only taking people with kids these days?"

"No," he said laughing, "Of course not. I was just surprised that a Mexican American female like yourself doesn't...."

"Not all of us have ten kids, you know," Medrano said with her voice dripping resentment.

What she hated most about stereotypes, Medrano thought, was that they confined people to boxes; and Medrano hated being boxed in and constrained. She hated staring at an eagle and being told that her spirit couldn't fly because only eagles were able to fly.

I am an eagle, she had decided. She had quieted those second thoughts as she finished answering the recruiter's questions. No more boxes, she thought.

By enlisting, she would stop herself from jumping into the next box waiting for her the box of sameness: go to the same job day after day; do the same things over and over; and climb the ladder little by little, inch by inch, leading a stagnating life.

This was the destiny thrust upon her because of the quiet and studious way she carried herself in school. She wasn't gregarious enough to be considered popular or exciting. The role of prom queen eluded her, but the role of intelligent nerd did not. Fellows did not want to date her. They were chasing the prom queen. All they wanted from her was help with their classes.

They never told her dirty jokes since that would be the same as telling them to their own mothers. She did not care about the jokes, but she did care about the fact that the world seemed divided in two. One side was for prom queens and the other for nerds.

She definitely belonged to that of the nerds, but she knew she was more than just smart. She had other attributes, like kindness and a good sense of humor. Her little sister Linda kept telling her she was attractive. She found it hard to believe until Linda dragged her to the mirror and told her to take a good look at herself. It was then she considered the possibility of actually being pretty. She could not be, however since the world was neatly divided; and beauty should not have brains. Yet the mirror was telling her differently, and it did not lie. This realization changed her a—bit there were no neat divisions. The world was indeed full of color. Not everything could be placed in neat boxes.

She began to change the destiny others wanted to create for her and felt relieved that she did not have to stay on "her side" of the world. She didn't have to be a stereotype or a statistic. She could have an exciting life, maybe even be beautiful, and do something out of the ordinary. She would eventually go to college, but it would have to wait until she saw what the rest of the world looked like. When she got off the bus and faced Fort Jackson, South Carolina, "this other side of the world" made everything somehow unreal to her. It was like a movie that had just started playing.

The new recruits were taken to the mess-hall where they were fed. Medrano would rather be sleeping than eating. Then they were taken into a little room and instructed to throw away any illegal items such as knives, no questions asked. In the room was a soldier and a dispenser to place the contraband. They also said the pledge of allegiance all over again. They had done this at the recruitment office at home. Finally, they were taken to the barracks.

Medrano realized she was in the Army. There were rows and rows of bunks with green bedspreads, just as in the movies. They were told to get rid of contraband such as candy, gum, and magazines. Outside there was a sergeant to speak to them.

Medrano was becoming impatient about getting her sleep. She

had never been a night owl. The female sergeant soon cleared up the sleep situation.

"Those of you with last names up to M's will not get any damn sleep tonight. We have to get you processed right now, and I don't want to hear any fucking complaining because I've been up all fucking night myself."

Medrano gasped. First of all, she had never heard two f-words used in the same sentence. She had never pulled an all-nighter. Maybe the other side of the world was not so interesting after all.

They were taken to the mess-hall and fed again, but the pale eggs were unappetizing. Medrano had never eaten powdered eggs.

From then on things became a blur for her. It was one thing after another with a lot of waiting. She waited to get her eyes checked, waited for blood to be sucked out from her, and waited for ten million vaccinations to be jabbed into her upper arms. It was the first time Medrano had heard the term, "hurry up and wait."

There were lines and lines of new recruits. She was convinced that the Army had turned her into a cow, and she was on a cattle call. When she went to get her uniforms, they were flung at her. The clothes were thrown at everyone, and each was yelled at if she did not pick them up fast enough and put them in her duffel bag. Medrano was directed into a room full of stalls. As she put on her clothes, she thought, I'm in the Army now. God save me.

The other females talked about enjoying the time in the reception station. Pretty soon their time there would be over, and they would be taken over by drill sergeants who would make them eat dust and tear out their bellies with pushups. Medrano, who never had been good in P.E., worried about this. P.E. was the class where she had received the worst grades. Exercising made her nauseous.

"Wait till the drill sergeant makes us do those man-style pushups. He'll whoop our asses," said one recruit.

Medrano's heart pumped harder at the thought.

"And this is zero week, Medrano. It's called zero week because it isn't counted. It's too easy to get counted. Yep, we're in this for seven weeks, not counting the time we're here," said another soldier.

Medrano just listened and listened. The first time she called her family, tears broke out; but she made her voice sound normal. She was not about to let her family know she was having second thoughts. She was going to take it like a woman, even if she was only eighteen, barely out of high school, and as terrified as a missionary in New York.

"Estoy bien, mama," her voice trembled as she told her mother she was fine. She only talked for a few minutes since she did not want the phone bill to skyrocket. As she hung up, she thought of all the miles that separated her from her family the miles that separated her and her former lifestyle.

Medrano blew her nose and wiped the last tears from her face. She would see her family again. Unfortunately, it would not be any time soon. Yes, she was in the Army for better or for worse and may death do them part.

To Medrano's chagrin, the remaining days at the reception station passed slowly. Some females kept telling her to enjoy it since the real horror was yet to come. She wanted it to come. She wanted to get it over.

Finally, the day arrived; and Medrano, along with all the other females, stood in formation. They waited for their drill sergeants to arrive and claim them. An uneasy silence permeated the air as they waited with anxiety riddled faces.

Medrano heard yelling behind her, but she did not dare turn her head. Her heart pounded, "It's them...it's them."

"The damn picnic is over. Your stay at the Holiday Inn is over!" the drill sergeants yelled.

A bead of perspiration glided down Medrano's face. This was it, she thought to herself, the moment of truth.

"Sergeant Acosta, have you ever seen a sorrier bunch of females?"

"No, I haven't, Sergeant Washington. These are a pitiful bunch, aren't they?"

"We'll be whipping you in tip-top shape. You belong to us now! You belong to Uncle Sam, and you'd better not forget it."

"The damn picnic is over. Your luxurious stay at the reception station is over. Now you're mine, and I'll smoke you asses till you become decent soldiers. Hey, soldier," he looked at a female next to Medrano, "do you know what it is to have your ass smoked?" She shook her head. "No? I'll have to smoke your ass till you get some sense."

Tears streamed down the female's face, while Medrano's throat quivered. She wanted to say something, but instinct told her not to. It was a good thing she did not. She soon would learn that smoking someone's ass was punishment through pushups. It was a slow and merciless torture that she would do better not knowing about until she absolutely had to know. Meanwhile, Medrano tried to send the crying female good thoughts.

"Aw look, Sergeant Washington, she's crying. Miss your parents, baby? Tears don't do a damn thing for us, so save them."

After a few more screams about the damn picnic being over, they were loaded and carted in cattle trucks. They were going to be taken to their new place of residence. Medrano decided that she better get used to being treated like an animal or else she'd be pretty mentally unstable until the nightmare ended in seven weeks.

Seven weeks!

AN ETERNITY!

First Week

Medrano's face was soaked when the troop started jogging. The reception station was a thing of the past—something she had gone through in another life. Now she was a soldier trying to get through PT and basic training since it was barely the first week. She let out a happy sigh not that she liked this activity. By the time they jogged, it meant the daily PT torture was almost over.

Through her peripheral vision, she made sure she was aligned with the soldiers at her sides. Medrano also made sure that she was on the same foot as everyone else. She certainly did not want the sergeant to snap at her. Besides, it was a hassle trying to jog in a disorganized group. The sergeant began to sing a cadence, and the troop sang after him:

Tiny bubbles,

in my drink,

make me happy,

and full of cheer.

Sweat ran over Medrano's shiny, light brown skin onto her grey shorts and T-shirt. They clung to her body. She hated when this happened since she already felt self-conscious about her body.

"Tiny bubbles in my drink, make me forget this damn, asshole Army," Peck sang.

Medrano managed to stifle a snicker. By now she was an expert in doing so. Her eyes stared straight ahead at the soldier in front of her, at her shiny, ebony neck. Perspiration was pouring down. Medrano wondered just how awful all of them smelled. She didn't have the power to smell perspiration anymore. Her nose had become accustomed to the stench.

They were nearing the barracks, and Medrano picked her feet up higher. She no longer dragged them since this was the last part of the nightmare. They ran past the soda and ice cream machines. Medrano looked longingly toward them. They were prohibited from using them. As they arrived at the barracks building, which was called Hollywood because it was the newest one, she looked up to where her particular barracks was located. It was on one of the top floors. The drill sergeant told them to stop running and to fall in line. They ran upstairs yelling, "Charlie, Charlie."

Charlie was the name of their company. Every company had a name that came directly from the military alphabet. A-Alpha, B-Bravo, C-Charlie, D-Delta and so forth. This alphabet was one of the things Medrano needed to learn in order to pass basic. Her knees wanted to buckle as she ran up the stairs. She had weak knees. Climbing stairs was especially difficult, but she tried to ignore the pain. Pain was something she had to learn to live with now. "No pain, no gain, no glory," came to her mind.

She walked into the barracks, and the variety of races hit her. She was still in awe of the different races represented in the Army. Sergeant Acosta had told her something that struck Medrano in a special way. He said there was only one color in the Army and that was green. Differences among the races were not as pronounced as soon as soldiers put on their uniforms, since all dressed the same.

They were going through the same experience. So at that time, they seemed more alike than different.

Medrano turned to a female next to her. "Hey, do you know what's next?"

"We practice marching for good ole Uncle Sam."

"Thanks for the info."

Medrano passed the first row of first squad bunks. She passed the second row of second squad bunks passed the grey lockers that divided first and second squad from third and fourth. She passed third squad, got to fourth, hung a left, and walked to her bunk. It was the seventh one down. She was close to the latrines, which were located in the back.

Medrano looked around to see that most of the females were undressing. She smiled, thinking of the word "females." As a civilian, she would have never thought of using the word, but the sergeants had ordered them to use it. They were no longer girls nor women. They were female soldiers.

Some of the females were busy taking off PT outfits and were dusting their lily-white, cotton bras with baby powder. They also put some powder in their matching white, cotton underwear, and their bodies. Baby powder was a must in the Army. Even if it didn't kill the stench, at least it gave them the illusion of doing so. As she was about to open her locker, she saw that Peck, her neighbor, was lying down and staring at the ceiling.

"What's wrong?" Medrano asked, looking at Peck's bright pink face. The bottom of her eyelids had a reddish tint, and she was wiping her paper-white skin with a hanky.

"Death is near. In fact, it's very, very near."

Medrano smiled. "How near is it?"

"Just one pushup away." Her voice and eyes turned ominous, and she stretched her palms toward the sky.

Medrano chuckled. "PT is awful, isn't it?"

"I bet this is what hell is like."

"Medrano, Peck, get your asses up and get dressed! You only have five minutes."

They looked toward the direction of the voice. It was Rogers, their squad leader. She was at the front of the row in the first bunk.

"Yes, master," said Peck and Medrano as they gave Rogers a dirty look. "I hate that bitch," Peck told Medrano as she got up and headed for her own locker.

Medrano nodded and went to her locker. She slid her dog tags out from her shirt and fingered them. She stared at her name printed in silver Medrano, Eliza. Sometimes she forgot she had a first name. A feeling of eeriness enveloped her as she thought about her entire identity etched on a metal trinket.

The tags also had her social security number, blood type, and religion printed on them. If she ever got killed in combat, her dog tags would prove who she was. She shivered at the thought of being in a body bag along with hundreds of others with only dog tags to separate who they were.

Medrano remembered she only had five minutes to get dressed, and she grabbed the locker key which was on the chain containing the dog tags. This was a nifty trick she learned from one of the females. She knew where her key was at all times. It was never in danger of getting lost, since she wore her dog tags everywhere, including the shower.

Medrano grabbed her camouflage uniform, which was crumpled up in one of the corners of the locker, and threw it on the bunk. She yanked off her shorts and shirt, grabbed baby powder, and shook it all over herself. Ivory powder flew every direction. It hit the floor, the locker, and the bedspread. Luckily it had not been a great amount. She threw the baby powder back in the locker and tossed the shorts and shirt after it. She silently prayed she would not get in trouble for the mess inside and outside her locker.

Usually she was not that careless, but sometimes she did not have a choice. It was either having a neat locker or not being late. She chose the second option. Tardiness was both her drill sergeants' pet peeve.

She threw the camouflage uniform on in record speed. By now, Medrano had the dress routine drilled into her head. First, she put on the green T-shirt and then the multi-green shaded pants. She made sure that all the buttons were buttoned, or she would be in trouble. They would smoke her derriere for certain. She made sure all her pockets and fly were buttoned. Next, she put on her multi-green shaded jacket. She folded it up at the sleeves, so she would not suffer heat stroke in the hot weather. She checked all her pocket buttons. Finally, she took her cap out of her pants' pocket. She always put it in the right pocket. Automatically her hand went to the left pocket to make sure her wallet was there.

She shut her locker, dusted off the bedspread, and ran out the door. As soon as she got outside, she put on her cap. It was against regulations to wear one inside and not to wear a cap outside. Most of the females were already in formation.

When she got to the bottom of the stairs, she looked nervously toward third platoon's formation area. The tenseness in her temples subsided when she saw that neither of her sergeants was there. She ran, or rather doubletimed it, to her area since walking was a big sin in the military. It was one of those privileges only afforded to civies. She went past the front of the formation area, to third platoon's and ran to her place in the fourth squad. There were already four, neat rows of soldiers all standing straight and quiet.

"Glad you could make it," Rogers whispered as Medrano ran past her.

Medrano shot her an angry glance. As she looked around, she saw she had been the only one in her squad missing. Still, Rogers was irritating.

Medrano wanted to say something back to Rogers, but she said nothing. She did not want the sergeants to find her talking in formation. That was another military sin. She just stared straight ahead and waited. She did not have to wait long before the sergeants arrived.

"A-tten-tion!" yelled Sergeant Acosta.

Everyone straightened up, put the heels of their feet together with their toes pointed outward, and dropped their hands to their sides. Their thumbs and first two fingers contracted to make an oval. They stood at attention, the base of all other movements.

Two females ran down the steps and into formation. Medrano squeezed her finger tips.

"Get the hell out of formation," Sergeant Washington said,

"Who the hell do you think you are being late like this? You think you're princesses or movie stars?"

One of the females was close to tears. "It's just that...."

Sergeant Washington looked at her with disgust. "I don't want any excuses, down!"

They immediately fell into the pushup position.

"Get up, get up, get up," the sergeant said.

They jumped up, and the sergeant made them go down again in the pushup position and then up again. The squat thrusts went on for about five minutes. They both burst into tears, but they kept doing as they were told.

"Get back in formation. Let this be a lesson to all of you third platoon. Don't you ever be late. Absolutely no excuses allowed. The only excuse I take is if you're dead. Next time something like this happens, I'm going to smoke all your asses to the ground. You'll be pushing Fort Jackson away. You've got to remember every second of your damned lives that you are no longer individuals. You're Uncle Sam's now. You work on the buddy system. If one of your buddies does something wrong, then all of you did something wrong. You are responsible for each other. Is that clear?!"

"Yes, sergeant," they rang in unison.

"Good. Right face!" They all turned right at the same time, "March." They marched beginning on the left foot as they were taught.

"Left face, march!"

For what seemed an eternity in the blazing sun, they practiced marching and changing directions every time the sergeants commanded. Medrano tried to keep aligned. Since she was uncoordinated, she was not sure she was aligned. All of them had to be in straight lines, and each had to be marching at the same time.

Sergeant Acosta started showing them other types of commands. Medrano kept rubbing her finger tips ever so slightly, since she could not bite her fingernails. She knew that marching would never be one of her favorite activities. She did not have a good memory for commands nor did she have grace. She was reminded constantly that she was good at the head stuff, or nerd stuff as she called it, but not physical stuff. After another eternity of soaking up cancerous sun rays, the sergeants finally let them go back to the barracks before lunch.

Medrano headed to the latrine. She passed all the talkative females and the ones lying on their bunks hyperventilating. She swung the latrine door open, found two empty stalls, and ran to the closest one. She quickly put toilet paper around the seat. It gave Medrano the willies thinking about all those behinds sitting on the toilets. Her insides emptied. She came out of the stall to find no sinks available.

Wall-to-wall females were washing their faces and rearranging their hair in tight buns. Females in the service did not have to cut their hair as males do, but they do have to keep it in a bun and orderly. Medrano's hand went to her own head to make sure every strand was in place.

"Go ahead and wash your hands," said a female who stepped aside to let her use the sink.

"Thanks."

Medrano smiled at her and washed her hands quickly. She did

not want to seem ungrateful for the nice gesture. She wiped her hands on her uniform and shook them as she walked out.

Medrano threw herself on her bunk. Peck was already spread across hers.

"You know that we'll get in trouble if the sergeants catch us lying on our asses," said Peck.

Medrano shot up. "We're not allowed to lie down between activities?"

"Nope. At least, I'm sure we're not. Those sergeants are real assholes."

When they first met, Medrano winced at Peck's vast use of the vulgar side of the English language. Now she was used to it.

"Then what are you doing lying down? Are you crazy? Do you want to get in trouble?"

Peck smiled wickedly. "Relax. The fucking sergeants aren't in their office."

"What if they return and find us lying down?"

"They won't find us lying down. The lockers that divide the barracks hide us from the entrance. By the time someone yells 'Man on the floor,' we'll get off the damn bunks before they even get a chance to see us."

"What if they forget to yell it?"

"Then they'll be in trouble for forgetting, and we'll hear the sergeants smoking their asses."

Medrano leaped to her bunk. "You've got an ingenious mind."

"Now if only that fuckhead, squad leader of ours doesn't come over and make us get up."

"Where is she?" Medrano asked, looking toward the first bunk.

"She's talking to the platoon guide, the mighty squad leader in charge of all other fuckhead, squad leaders." Medrano sat up. "I don't think I'll ever get any rest around here."

"Rogers will probably be back any minute with the sole intention of making our lives miserable."

Medrano shook her head and suddenly had a vision of the floor beneath her bunk.

"Grab your pillow, Peck." Medrano slid under her bunk with her pillow.

"What are...."

"Rogers can't see us under here unless she's doing the same thing we are."

Peck snickered and slid under her bunk. "You've got fucking brains."

"Just because I have problems doing the physical stuff doesn't mean I'm stupid," Medrano stated.

"You know what your problem is, Med?"

Medrano rolled her eyes. "What is my problem, Peck?"

"You take this shit too seriously."

"What are you talking about?"

"Basic. All they are doing is playing mind games with us to weed out those who won't be able to handle a fucking war." Peck's face suddenly grew soft, which was an unusual expression for her. "You've got to hang on to yourself in here and make yourself tough," she said as she put her hand over her heart.

"And laugh. Laugh and laugh until nothing hurts."

Peck's eyes grew glassy. It seemed to Medrano that Peck wasn't talking to her but to herself. Peck was lost in another world, and Medrano wondered where it was.

"But...," Medrano started to say.

"I can handle a fucking war or anything else that comes my way." Peck said as her "Don't-mess-with-me" expression came back.

"I'm sure...."

"I'm going to kick this peacetime Army right in the ass."

"Peacetime what?"

Peck grew impatient, "Peacetime Army. We entered the Army during peacetime and not during wartime."

The word peacetime fascinated Medrano. "Oh. But...."

"At least you're not as bad as her," said Peck, pointing at Morningstar. "She can't march worth shit, and she can't even do half a pushup."

Medrano looked at Morningstar who was by herself as usual and was practicing doing pushups next to her bunk. Morningstar was Native American, and Medrano wondered if she had been raised on a reservation. She was curious about her, but Morningstar usually kept to herself.

"She tries very hard," Medrano said, "Morningstar doesn't sleep like we do during off time."

"But she's an even bigger weakling than you are."

Medrano's eyes strayed to the soldiers around her. Some were talking, and others were re-reading letters. Clad in their camouflage uniforms, they tried to make believe they were exactly where they wanted to be when they really wanted to be with parents, boyfriends, and other loved ones. At these moments, weakness and bravery were awfully close to each other in Medrano's eyes. It had become as easy to cry when reading a letter as it was to bite one's lip while grinning and bearing it during PT.

"Everyone's got weaknesses." Medrano stated.

"I don't!"

"So you're a perfect human being?"

"I just don't let any fucking fears make me weak."

"Aren't you ever scared, Peck?"

"No."

"There isn't some fear inside you being covered up with laughter?" asked Medrano, trying to get Peck back to the place she had been earlier when her blue eyes turned glassy.

For a split second, Peck's eyes showed surprise. Then they grew angry and closed off.

"Fear is for cowards. I'm not a coward!"

"But...."

"Time to go to fucking lunch," Peck said as she sat up.

Figuring Peck out was impossible, thought Medrano as she pulled herself up. After pushing their pillows into the covers, they ran through the doors, down the stairs, and to their formation area. Sergeant Acosta marched them over to the mess-hall where they formed a single line outside. Medrano fixed her eyes straight ahead. She stood straight and at parade-rest with her hands behind her back, one on top of the other, and her elbows pointing to each side.

This position made her, along with everybody else, resemble a bird preparing for flight. At the pit of her stomach, she felt she was more like a bird with clipped wings. Each time the line moved, Medrano got into attention before moving forward. Then she had to stand at attention again before taking the parade-rest position. All this seemed pretty silly to her. Why did they have to go through all this mumbo jumbo?

The line inside the mess-hall looked pretty much like the one outside. They still had to stand at parade-rest, look straight ahead, and not talk to anyone until they picked up their trays. Medrano once again thought about their looking like birds with their elbows sticking out and hands folded neatly behind them.

A sergeant was right there waiting for them to make a mistake. He was Drill Sergeant Grimes from second platoon. Rumor was that he made hamburger patties out of soldiers. He walked up and down with a stupid grin on his face. Each one of them tried to focus ahead, so they would not have to see his grin in their peripheral vision.

As he passed by Medrano, she could feel splotches of nervous heat on her skin. His eyes dissected every soldier, seemingly penetrating the uniforms. Medrano was overcome with feelings of being dirty. She wondered why she felt this way since she couldn't even see his eyes. How would she know if they were lustful? Maybe he was such a despicable character that she wanted to make him into a lascivious creep too.

"I've never seen such a bunch of losers!" Sergeant Grimes screamed as spit shot out of his mouth.

Same to you, buddy, thought Medrano. Although getting verbally abused was now part of her life, it was taking a long time to get used to it.

"You'll never make it through this Army." He stood in front of one soldier who was in front of Medrano, challenging her to eyeball him. She would not oblige.

Medrano almost laughed out loud. To see a sergeant fail at intimidation was tremendous. The moment of ecstasy did not last long however. The sergeant was not happy with the soldier's lack of fear. He grabbed the soldier's large chignon.

"Your hair is too damn long. You'll have to cut it. Did you hear me?" Sergeant Grimes asked.

"Yes, sergeant," she managed to choke out, as tears fell like a waterfall from her eyes.

Medrano was convinced that drill sergeants were subhuman species obtained by the armed forces from faraway planets where happiness was prohibited. "Next time I see you, I want to see that shit cut. Am I making myself clear?"

"Yes, sergeant." The words were barely audible.

The soldier grabbed her tray, and Medrano followed her. A light rattling sound reached Medrano's ears. She looked down to see the female's hands shaking so hard that her tray was banging against the metal under it. Those trembling hands entered the special part of Medrano's memory bank reserved for moments that would be with her the rest of her life, such as her graduation and her mama's painful hysterectomy.

Medrano pointed to the food she wanted and took her seat at the first-available table she saw. The chicken and the peas stuck in her throat, so she drank big gulps of milk. Peck sat across from her and looked down pretending to cut the chicken.

"Do you believe those pigs?" Peck whispered, making sure the sergeants eating at the front table did not see her move her lips.

"Sometimes I wonder about their humanity," said Medrano, making believe she was chewing instead of talking.

Medrano felt a certain satisfaction that she and Peck were fooling the sergeants. All the soldiers had mastered the art of being barely audible and using their lips minimally. The sergeants had made it very clear that the mess-hall was a place to eat and not a recreation area. Medrano shuddered to think about what would be done to them if the cadre found out about their means of communication.

"Pigs," whispered Peck.

They didn't talk to each other after that. Their newfound talent could get them in trouble, and that was one thing they did not need. Medrano gobbled down her food. This was another talent she had learned in the Army. Eating fast was a must since the sergeants had made it very clear that there were a lot of mouths to feed in this one mess-hall.

Finished, she took her plate over to a giant trash can, dumped the food she had not eaten, and put her tray with the other ones in front of the wash room. She grabbed her cap from her pocket and prayed that when she went outside, she would not see any officers. She was scared of them more than she was of sergeants. They had more power. She was grateful that she did not have to salute a sergeant. For them a simple "good afternoon, sergeant," would do; but for an officer, it became more complicated.

For an officer she would have to slow down her pace from doubletiming it right before reaching the officer. Then she would stand at attention when she stood in front of and salute while saying, "good afternoon, ma'am/sir." Medrano would have to wait until the officer saluted her before she could put her hand down. Then she would go on her merry way, doubletiming it until she got to the barracks. It was a long procedure; and Medrano knew she would mess up, given the opportunity. She prayed that the opportunity would never arise.

Medrano opened the mess-hall door, put on her cap, and started doubletiming it. She saw trouble in the distance. An officer was there all right, smoking some poor misguided soul. You've gotten her, buddy; but you are definitely not going to get me, she thought. She ran into the latrine for females located beside the mess-hall.

She was amazed at the number of females there. All the stalls were full and so were the sinks. Some were sitting on the floor.

"Hey you."

Medrano wasn't sure if she should answer. "Are you talking to me?"

"No, I'm talking to the sink."

Medrano stared coldly at the female. "Continue talking to it then."

"Was that asshole officer still out there?" asked another soldier.

At that, the latrine grew silent as if everyone was waiting for the answer. Medrano finally caught on. Everyone there was doing exactly the same thing she was hiding out like a coward.

"He was still out there," Medrano said.

"Was he still dogging that female?"

Dogging was a new word for Medrano, but she guessed it meant the same thing as smoking someone.

"She was still pushing Fort Jackson away."

"Shit," several females said in unison.

Someone came out of one of the stalls, and Medrano quickly took it. She really had to go. This always happened when her nerves were on the blink. This time she didn't cover the toilet seat with paper. She urinated while practically standing up. It made her uneasy to think that the water coming out of her was so yellow. Another soldier had told her this was because the military put something called 'Salt Peter' in the food to quell their carnal desires. When finished, she looked to make sure she hadn't missed. She hated messy toilets, she practiced the golden rule. With everything fine, she flushed and walked out of the stall.

The latrine was now practically empty. Medrano sighed, relieved that it was probably safe to leave. She quickly washed her hands and ran outside.

Her nerves didn't stop jumping until she got to the stairs of her barracks. Medrano ran up; and as she walked through the double doors, she wiped sweat beads from her upper lip. Breathing deeply, she stood there for a while, listening to the different voices.

"We practice marching in ten minutes, people!" Walker, the platoon guide, yelled.

"Great," Medrano mumbled under her breath.

"Doing good, Medrano," Walker said as Medrano walked past her. "Keep it up girl."

"Thank you, Walker."

Medrano really liked her. Walker's dark, brown skin always glowed with enthusiasm, and she never held back compliments. Medrano smiled as she walked to her locker and poured some baby powder down her shirt.

"Take it easy on that stuff," Peck said.

Medrano jumped, and baby powder landed everywhere. She searched for Peck but could not find her.

"Down here."

Medrano looked down and saw Peck under her bunk. "How long have you been down there?"

"I just got here."

After cleaning up the baby powder, Medrano grabbed her pillow and hit the floor. She was about to speak when she noticed that Peck was talking to her neighbor who was also on the floor. The activity was catching on. Medrano shut her eyes, trying to drown out her environment. Her mind numbed, and she drifted off to sleep.

A scene erupted in her mind. She was suddenly in the deep wilds of the jungle. The color green looked as if it wanted to bite her. She could not escape the color even in her dreams. The smell of danger filled her nostrils. She looked around her and felt chaos trembling in her being. Vines were intertwined, and silent movement was everywhere. Would the terrors that caused these movements spring up and kill her? Beads of sweat glided down her forehead, and her hands shook.

At a distance Medrano heard dogs barking, and a sense of fear enveloped her. Some evil was out to get her. It's vibrations quivered deep inside of her. She ran but could not move anywhere. It was like running in place. Dogs were getting nearer and nearer, and she could not get out of there.

Medrano tried to wake from her nightmare; but, like a pit bull, it would not let her go. Screams caught in her throat. Finally, she was able to move; but she did not get very far before she stepped on a trap and her feet were pulled out from under her. She hung from a tree with her feet tied together with rope. The sweat from her body slid to the ground. She waited silently.

A figure came into sight. It was the officer she had seen smoking the female outside the mess-hall. He had a victorious grin on his face. She tried screaming again, but nothing came out of her mouth. The officer was getting closer and so were the dogs. Then she saw that the dogs had the faces of her drill sergeants. She looked toward the sky hoping for help.

"Med, Med!"

She could hear her name being called. Help was near, but it better hurry.

"Med, get the hell up! We're going to be late." Peck exclaimed.

Medrano woke but could not speak for a few seconds. She looked around wildly.

"What's wrong? You look like you've been scared out of your fucking wits," said Peck.

Medrano found her voice. "I had a nightmare."

"What about?"

"This!" Medrano exclaimed as she looked around the barracks.

"What?"

"I had a nightmare about this place and about death."

"You've been dreaming about death? You'd better stop taking things so seriously, Med. Even your dreams are being polluted with your anxieties. You'd better be fucking careful."

"Yeah," she said trembling. "Let's get out of here before my nightmare comes true."

They got out from under the bunks and ran out to formation and practiced marching. Medrano kept her eyes on the female directly in front of her. She did not want her eyes to stray and see her sergeants. She especially did not want to see the officer who had been in her nightmare.

After marching practice, they were taken into a lecture room where the females from all four platoons were seated.

"What is this all about?" someone asked Medrano.

"I have no idea," she said and promptly sipped up. She turned to look at the female who had asked her. It was the same one who had been told to cut her hair in the mess-hall. Her black, shiny hair was still long.

Around her she caught the puzzled looks of her peers. They were also curious as to what this was concerning. The last time they had been there, they were shown a film on rape, and how to prevent it and report it.

A film began. As it rolled away, she realized it was about foot problems. Her stomach took a dive when she saw green feet.

"I know the Army loves green," the female with the long hair elbowed Medrano and whispered, "but this is ridiculous. Yuck."

Medrano nodded her head and held her stomach. She checked the female's name over her breast pocket. It was García. I could've sworn she was African American, Medrano thought, looking at García's ebony skin.

"Change your socks twice a day," the man in the film said. "Use baby powder. You don't want your feet to end up looking like this."

A pair of feet were shown with sores the size of moon craters. This time the decor wasn't green. It was black.

"What's wrong, Medrano?" Sergeant Acosta asked.

"Nothing, sergeant."

"Like hell." He walked away laughing. Medrano shivered, remembering her dream.

"Couldn't they have done this in a cartoon?" Medrano asked García.

"No, that would be too much of a decent thing for the Army to do."

"You're right. They can't get the reputation of being nice."

They saw a sergeant eyeing them and clammed up.

After the film was over, they were allowed to go back to the barracks to wait for dinner. Instead of sitting on her bunk, Medrano sat on the floor—she did not want to mess up her bunk. She studied from a little white book.

"Medrano, what the fuck are you doing?" asked Peck.

"I'm studying my smart book."

"What the hell for? None of us is going to learn anything from those damn things. Might as well sleep," she said, as she dived under her bunk.

"I need to learn my general orders."

"Suit yourself."

Medrano concentrated on the little book. She needed to learn her general orders in case a sergeant or officer would ask what they were while she was on fireguard duty. Boy, did she hate fireguard duty. It interfered with her sleep, and sleep was one thing she hated doing without. To her dismay, she would have to do it every four nights because each squad alternated every night. Medrano would only get five hours of sleep on fireguard nights and felt like a zombie the next morning.

The night was divided into two-hour shifts, and two females had to be on every shift. One female guarded the double door. The other walked around the barracks, making sure lockers were locked and soldiers were covered. The females had to have their blankets on; if officers or sergeants inspected during the night, they would not catch them in their undies. Armed with their trusty flashlights, these brave fireguards guarded their territory. Most of the lights were turned off at 9 p.m.

Medrano repeated her three general orders out loud again and again as if repeating a rosary. "I will guard everything within the limits of my post and quit my post only when properly relieved. I will obey my special orders and perform all my duties in a military manner. I will report violations of my special orders, emergencies, and anything not covered in my instructions to the commander of the relief."

Soon she got tired of repeating them and started leafing through her little white book, her smart book. It contained everything she needed to learn in basic training. They were given to all soldiers in basic. Classes and demonstrations would be given on the subjects in the book. At the end of the training, they would be tested.

She stopped at the page on first aid. That was a subject she had always wanted to learn. She flipped to the weapons part. Could it be that she, gentle Medrano, would learn how to fire one of those rifles? If she had already learned, maybe she would have fired one at the officer in her nightmare.

She concentrated on her general orders again. By repeating them, somehow she felt more in control of her life. The ability to learn them lay solely on her.

"Med, would you shut the fuck up? Some of us are trying to nod into fairyland where there are no asshole sergeants and where no green exists. You catch my drift?" Peck asked.

"I'm sorry. I didn't realize I was making so much noise

"Just put a tupperware lid on it."

"All right, all right."

"Good, now shut the fuck up," Peck said turning her face away from Medrano.

She put her smart book in her side pant pocket and got up to walk around. Getting yelled at was not at the top of her list of exciting things to experience.

She walked toward the latrine where she found García combing her long, black tendrils over a sink. She debated whether to talk to her and find out whether she was going to cut her hair. Sometimes her curious nature get the best of her, and she knew curiosity killed the cat.

"Hi, how's it going?" she asked; letting the cat fend for itself. Nothing was going to get between her and her quest for knowledge. Was her curiosity not part of her intelligence?

"Hi," García smiled.

"Survive the ugly-feet movie?" she asked, getting near the dark haired Rapunzel.

"Not only did I survive, but my stomach survived too."

"I saw what that jerk sergeant did to you in the mess-hall. If someone had asked me to cut my hair, I would've died. Especially if my hair was as pretty as yours."

"Thanks. He's a jerk, isn't he? He just grabbed me by the hair and almost pulled all of it out," García said, anger flaming in her voice.

"Are you going to cut it?" Medrano could hear the cat meowing.

"Sergeant Acosta told me I didn't have to cut it."

"Really?" Medrano's eyes widened and did not leave García's face, "I just can't believe it."

"In fact, the sergeant said that no asshole from another platoon would tell his soldiers what to do."

"And I thought all those sergeants were in cahoots with one another to make our lives miserable."

"I guess not."

Medrano grew pensive for a while. "Think there's a remote possibility they may be human? That they care for us?"

"I don't know. Maybe just a remote possibility. The remotest, of course."

They were silent while trying to swallow this new reality. Life held many surprise turns. García put her hair up in a bun. Medrano stared at it. She had always wanted long hair but her hair only grew to her shoulders. Split ends prevented it from growing longer. She touched her shiny bob and sighed.

"Let's go sit on my bunk," García said.

"Give me a minute," Medrano dashed into one of the stalls and again remained almost standing up. Bingo, she had not missed.

Medrano followed García to her bunk which was in third squad and toward the back. It was even farther back than Medrano's, but Medrano could see her bunk from García's. She could also see that Peck was fast asleep.

"Don't you think those sergeants are too rough on us?" Medrano asked.

"Definitely. I hear that they're just about the toughest sergeants around."

"I wouldn't be surprised."

"I'd rather have them as our sergeants than...."

"Grimes!" Medrano exclaimed.

"If I tell you something, do you promise not to tell anyone?" García asked, lowering her voice and looking all around her. "I'm good at keeping secrets."

"Grimes gives me a real bad feeling, Medrano."

"Me too."

"You know when he grabbed my hair?" asked García.

"Yes."

"There was something about the way he touched me," said García uncomfortably.

"Do you think...."

"Let's not talk about this anymore. It's probably my imagination anyway," García said.

"But...."

"The important thing is that he's not our sergeant."

"Thank goodness," said Medrano.

"Our sergeants may be tough, but it's because they want us to be the best platoon in the battalion."

Medrano's eyes grew small. "Yeah and they don't care if they kill us in the process. They're heartless."

"I guess that in a war you have to be heartless. That's the way you're able to kill people."

Medrano stared at the palm of her hand very intently. "You go bam, bam, turn off your emotions, and hope those people never breathe again."

"I hope we're never in a war," García said as she stared into space.

"Imagine getting killed, and all your identity will be left on this," Medrano said pulling out her dog tags and fingering them. "You'd be one in many." She bounced the shiny, silver metal on the palm of her hand. The fluorescent lights hit it, making it sparkle.

"That's scary." García touched her own dog tags through her shirt.

"That's not the only thing scary around here."

García chuckled. "Yeah, it's something surviving those creatures they call drill sergeants."

"I miss my freedom so much."

"I miss home."

"Where's home?" Medrano asked.

"San Antonio," García said, giving it a Spanish pronunciation.

"Are you also African...."

"My dad's Mexican from Monterrey, and my mom's African American," she stated proudly.

García was someone she could relate to culturally. Being so far away from home made Medrano search for pieces of it here and there. Finding someone with a similar background brought her closer to it.

"Where are you from, Medrano?"

"I'm from a little town in New Mexico, Sunland Park—which is close to El Paso."

They heard the abrupt sound of running feet and turned toward the noise.

"I guess it's time to go eat our caviar and champagne," Medrano said.

García nodded. Both doubletimed it outside, got into formation, and stood promptly at attention like good soldiers. Medrano almost audibly gasped when she saw Sergeant Grimes go toward García.

"Didn't I tell you to get rid of this shit?" He grabbed her hair.

Medrano could sense García's frustration. Even though she could not see García's face, Medrano could feel her vibrations. She decided that if she ever had the opportunity, she would shove a green chile, a big one, up the sergeant's rear end. Right between the cheeks, Medrano thought. She almost jumped when she heard Sergeant Acosta's voice. She had forgotten he was in the room.

"The truth of the matter, Sergeant Grimes, is that I told her she didn't have to cut her hair. Females don't have to as long as they keep it orderly and in a bun."

"I'm very well aware of that, Sergeant Acosta. Her damn hair sticks out too much from the bun. It's too long, and her cap doesn't fit right because of it."

"Chill out, sergeant. I'll handle my own platoon."

"Okay, Sergeant Acosta. You can do whatever you want. It is your platoon," he said and walked away.

Medrano's mouth gaped. If she had not witnessed this act of kindness from her drill sergeant, she would not have believed it. García held her head high, and Medrano inhaled deeply. Life was not so bad after all even in the Army.

After she got her tray, she sat across from García, who gave her a grin from ear-to-ear. Medrano looked down at her tray and whispered. "Good thing to know that the remote possibility they're human is growing." She stuffed some mashed potatoes in her mouth and raised her head.

García chewed her food and talked at the same time. "They may even pass the human being test now."

They shut up after that. The sergeant's bizarre "human-like" behavior could end just like that if he caught them talking.

They finished their food, doubletimed it back to the barracks, and learned ecstatically that their hard day was over. Of course, they couldn't do what they wanted to after hours as in a normal job. The military was a twenty-four hour deal. Still, they enjoyed the time, enjoyed simply not being ordered to do something.

Medrano grabbed her second pair of boots and her shoe-shine kit and went over to García's bunk. They both began polishing their boots. Medrano started at the front of the boot, first making small, circular movements with a rag. This was the part she would fail because she would get impatient in seconds and start making large, circular movements instead.

Consequently, her boots were never as shiny as she wanted them. She wished she could get her boots to shine like mirrors, so she always promised that the next time she would get them like that. But she never did.

After making the circular movements, she used the brush to give them that extra gleam. This was her favorite part of shining boots. She gave them some of her gusto. After that, she took a cloth (when it became ragged, she replaced it with a baby diaper) and ran it over the boots by sashaying it sideways.

"You've got a lot more patience than I do when it comes to shining these things," Medrano commented.

"I just like to see them gleam."

Medrano glanced at García who was still on her first boot. She was already on her second. "I guess I'm too impatient for my own good."

García chuckled. "I used to polish my papa's shoes all the time."

"Oh, so you've got experience. I wish I could say the same, but the closest I came to polishing shoes was wiping my sister's and my heels with toilet paper," she said. "I sure miss my sister."

"Join the club, Medrano. You know one of the things I miss the most?"

"What is that?"

"Eating something that looks halfway like food?" asked García.

"Army chow isn't that bad."

"Not that bad? Have you seen those white-powdered eggs they serve us in the mornings?"

"They do kinda lack flavor," said Medrano.

"You better believe they lack flavor. And everything else lacks flavor too."

"The food isn't that bad. We just miss our mother's home cooking," Medrano stated.

García looked dreamily ahead. "I sure do miss Mama's cooking. I'll tell you what I miss. I miss cheese grits. I would also give my right arm to get a hold of a taco right now."

"Yeah, a taco with chile and a side order of frijoles—pink, plump, juicy, pinto beans."

"How about homemade tortillas?"

"Don't say anymore, García; or I'll dream about those tortillas all night."

García stood up. "There's no place like home, no place like home," she stood up and tapped her feet together like Dorothy in the Wizard of Oz. "It didn't work."

"No, we're still in this nightmare." Medrano shoved both her boots aside and started putting together her shoe polishing kit. García sat down and started on her second boot.

"Life's a bitch, Medrano."

"And then you die."

"Isn't that the truth, García?"

"Do you wish you had never joined?"

Medrano grimaced. "I guess I complain too much. The truth is if I had to do it all over again, I'd do the same thing."

"It's better than being a cashier at some store. That's what I used to do after school. I guess I'd still be working there if I hadn't joined. What would you be doing?"

"Financially struggling through college," said Medrano.

"College is expensive, isn't it?"

"Yes. The good thing about the Army is that it's a way to pay for it and see the world at the same time."

"Do you think we'll get to go to Europe?" asked García.

"I'm positive. I heard they especially send singles overseas. We'll be gallivanting off to Europe in no time."

"Think we'll get some of those romantic Italian men to whisper sweet nothings in our ears?" asked García.

"Heck, I'd be happy if they'd scream those sweet nothings on the subway, as long as it is a man without a stitch of green on," Medrano said, fingering her uniform and singing. "Mama, mama can't you see." García joined in, "what this Army's done to me? Took away my bright blue jeans, now I'm wearing Army greens."

They stopped abruptly when they heard someone yelling.

"Everyone to the front! Everyone to the front!"

"What do they want this time?" frowned Medrano, "I thought we were through for the day."

They ran to the front of Roger's bunk. It was Sergeant Acosta yelling.

"I'm going to teach all of you to prepare for locker inspections. Listen well because I'm only explaining this once."

He showed them where everything went, from toothpaste to socks. When he got to the underwear, he held one up by the tip as if he did not want to touch it.

"Sergeant Acosta," Rogers said, "those are a new pair of underwear. I haven't worn them yet." There was a roar of laughter.

"I don't blame him for not wanting to touch them. One touch and off you go to the clinic for a rabies shot," Peck whispered to Medrano.

Medrano giggled. "You're too much."

"Medrano, Peck, I see you talking. Drop and give me ten."

They grimaced and dropped at the same time. Neither did the

pushups well, but they tried.

"One sergeant, two sergeant...," they said in unison until they reached ten.

"Consider yourselves lucky because today you caught me in a good mood. Next time I'll really smoke your asses."

They got up with shining faces. Medrano sighed. Even though doing ten pushups was not the easiest thing in the world, she knew she had gotten off easy.

"All buttons have to be buttoned," Sergeant Acosta continued with a uniform in hand.

García gave Medrano a look that said, "I'm glad it wasn't me." Medrano gave her back a look of, "I'll never do that again. It was as painful and humiliating as it looked." Medrano glanced at Peck, who was smiling and as happy as could be. "Didn't anything get to that girl?" she wondered. Peck grinned as if to say, "We got caught but that asshole sergeant did not do much to us."

Medrano resolved that when she got out of the Army, she would put on her resume: mindreader, experience seven weeks in basic training where often the only means of communication was the noodle.

"Make sure your lockers end up looking exactly like this. We may call a surprise inspection at any moment."

Medrano caught García's eye. Her expression said the same thing. "Something else to worry about."

"Now go fix your lockers," the sergeant commanded.

They ran to their lockers as if the sergeant himself was chasing after them. Medrano opened her locker and stared sadly into it.

"What's wrong, Med? Can't deal with perfection in your locker?" asked Peck.

"This reminds me of my mama making me clean my room. I hate organizing things. I can never find anything after I clean up."

Medrano began arranging her locker just as the sergeant had shown them. After she finished, she called Rogers to make sure everything was perfect.

"Looks fine to me, Medrano."

"Are you sure?"

"I already said it looks fine!"

"I just don't want to end up having my behind smoked!" Medrano exclaimed.

Roger's stern glare turned soft. She put one hand on Medrano's shoulder. "It looks fine."

"Thanks."

Rogers nodded and walked off.

Why are you asking that bitch for her opinion?" asked Peck.

"She is the squad leader. Besides, she isn't that bad."

"Yes she is. Why do you think she was chosen to be a squad leader? She's a miniature drill sergeant if you ask me."

"Nonetheless, she is our squad leader."

"Stop reminding me of that. Oh, well who gives a fuck. It'll all be over in a couple of weeks," she said yawning and on her bunk.

Medrano shook her head and grabbed her shorts and shirt and headed for the latrine. Soap and water would be a welcome treat.

When she got to the shower room, it was practically full of nude females. She took off all her clothes except for her dog tags. The first time she took a shower with other females in the reception station, she died of embarrassment. Her body looked nothing like the ones in the nudie magazines, and she was protective of her body. She hadn't let her most beloved boyfriend near it. She had had a total of two boyfriends, and neither had seen or touched her private parts.

It wasn't that Medrano's virginity meant that much to her. She didn't carry her unbroken hymen like a badge of honor which she would present to her groom like a prize on her wedding day. There were several reasons she hadn't had sexual intercourse yet. First, sexually transmitted diseases terrified her—especially AIDS. Second, babies at this point in her life would prevent her from seeing the world; and she was smart enough to know that no form of birth control was 100 percent foolproof. Third, she sensed that too often there were power games involved in sex; and she was too young to know how to play. Medrano hated the thought of anyone making a fool or taking advantage of her, so she avoided it. For these reasons, her physical self stayed closed for business; and she shielded her body so much that a communal shower was extremely uncomfortable at best.

Medrano's modesty soon died in the Army. She realized that no other female's body looked like a centerfold's either. Instead, she focused on more important issues. She finished showering and dressed. As she walked out of the latrine, she heard the sergeant's voice.

"Mail call! Mail call!"

Medrano ran to her locker, dumped her toiletries, and ran to the front where the sergeant was standing. She prayed that there would be a letter for her. At the last mail call, there had been nothing. She had run to one of the stalls in the latrine, so no one would see her crying. No one in her family was a great letter writer.

She heard names and more names and shrieks of joy, but there was nothing for her. Her fingers went to her mouth, and she started gnawing on her fingernails again. In front of her, Dekan was tearing open a letter, and Medrano could feel her excitement. Dekan looked as if she had forgotten where she was and melted into the world of the letter. From where Medrano stood, she could see the words clearly.

I wish I could be with you to tell you how much I love you. No other girl can even begin to compare to you. I can't wait to see you and make love to you all night. I fantasize about you all day and night. Your big, voluptuous....

Suddenly Medrano realized what she was doing and moved away. A wave of guilt gnawed inside of her.

"Medrano."

It took a second to register in Medrano's head that she had received a letter.

"Here, sergeant." She pushed through the crowd and snatched the letter from the sergeant's hand. The sergeant gave her an odd look, and everyone laughed.

She stepped back and looked at the front of the envelope. It was from her sister.

"Medrano."

She stopped ripping the envelope and stared at the sergeant. Could he be playing a cruel joke, or had she received two letters on the same night?

"Medrano, don't you want your letter?" he asked sternly.

"Yes, sergeant," Medrano's voice squeaked. Again, she pushed her way to the front.

"This time don't knock my fingers out of their sockets to get your letter, all right?" There was another roar of laughter.

Medrano herself grew hot and hoped her brown skin would cover the red flush that passed over her face. She stood in front of the sergeant and extended her palm. By this time, the females were almost on the floor with laughter. Medrano began laughing too. She had learned to laugh at herself. Otherwise, it only made matters worse.

The letter was from her cousin Lillian who was working at a minimum wage job; trying to earn money for college. Medrano walked back to her bunk after mail call was over.

She read the letter from her sister first. Linda was a year younger and in her senior year in high school. Tears welled in her eyes as she read the innocent pitfalls of teenage years. After all, it had not been that long since she had experienced the same things. Linda, like Medrano, had been labeled a "nerd" and had her heart broken by many a fellow who lusted for a cheerleader. Medrano remembered a time when the loneliness of feeling different from the other top students, in their lives of popularity and ease, overwhelmed and strangled her.

"Crybaby, crybaby," Peck said.

"Doesn't anything ever get to you?"

Peck laid down on her bunk. "No." She turned away and began talking to the female on the other side.

Medrano was getting used to Peck's strange personality. She opened her second letter, hoping she would not succumb to feelings of depression.

Lillian wrote about all the events happening at home—the new movies, the latest gossip, and her job. Medrano began daydreaming about what it would be like to be Lillian, to have that sort of freedom. What was it like not to have to wait in lines, not to get screamed at, and not to have to wear green?

Medrano snapped out of it. She was succumbing to depression. Hadn't she told García just moments ago that if she had to do it all over again, she would do the same thing? She wiped the tears from her eyes. The least she could do for herself was keep away the doubts. Stop dwelling on whether the choice she had made was good or bad. She would save herself from her own worst enemy. She put away the letters, breathed deeply, and hoped she could pull off the enormous task of not feeling sorry for herself.

"You know what your problem is, Med?" Peck's voice cut through Medrano's thoughts and startled her.

"What?"

"Your problem is...."

Medrano regained her composure. "You."

"Me?!" she exclaimed.

"You and your criticisms of everybody. Just because you think life is an easy glide. A joke!"

Peck jumped up from her bunk and grabbed Medrano's shoulders. "A joke! You think you're the only one with problems?" Peck bit her lip as if she had already said too much. She took her hands off Medrano's shoulder and returned to her bunk. "Your problem is your teenage hormones are fucking up. It happens to all of us. Goodnight." Peck jumped under her blankets and shut her eyes.

Just when Medrano thought she was getting to know what flowed below Peck's rough exterior, she would shut off like a faucet. Medrano covered herself with her blankets and checked her Timex watch. It was 8:45. Bedtime was 9:00, but she decided to think in military time. In the a.m. zeros were added, so 4:00 a.m. would become 0400 hours. In the p.m. the numbers were counted after twelve and zeros were added. For example, 1:00 p.m. was 1300 hours, 2:00 p.m. was 1400; and so on. Medrano looked at her watch again and counted, so 9:00 p.m. was 2100 hours. She had fifteen minutes until that time.

Medrano's skin tingled with the thought of sleeping fifteen extra minutes. She had to get her z's where she could. Basic was not going to get any easier.

She felt another ray of happiness when she realized that the next day was Sunday. The soldiers would be allowed to sleep an extra hour. They did not have to wake up until 5:00 a.m., 0500 hours. Also, the sergeant had told them that they would be allowed to go to church. Peck told her that it was illegal for them not to let them go. It was going to be nice to be doing a non-basic training activity for a change. With that Medrano drifted off to sleep.

The serenity of sleep did not last long. Soon she began to dream. This time she was not in the jungle. She was outside the barracks, and Sergeant Acosta was in front of her.

"Down," he said.

Medrano got in the pushup position and began pushing Fort Jackson away.

"You won't be going to church tomorrow, soldier. In fact, you will wake up an hour before everybody and scrub toilets with a toothbrush! Are you listening, you ass wipe of a soldier?"

He took an M-16 rifle, such as the ones Medrano had seen soldiers in other battalions carry on their right shoulders, and pointed it at her. She wanted to scream; but, just like before, nothing came out of her mouth. Like the other nightmare, this one did not want to let go of her. In the world outside her dream, she wanted to kick; but her body would not move. In her dream, she could not stop doing pushups, even when he cocked the M-16.

Suddenly, the world seemed to tremble; and she woke up. She didn't open her eyes. She was trying to figure out if she was awake or still having a nightmare. A distant light filtered through her eyelids and brought her back to awareness. She opened her eyes and was relieved to see no sergeant next to her. She looked around and realized that the light was a fireguard's flashlight.

She squinted to check the time. It was 2:00 a.m., 0200 hours, and so quiet. For a moment, she shoved the nightmare to the back of her mind and listened to the peacefulness. Silence was not something she took for granted anymore. There was no sergeant screaming, no cadence, no sounds of people shining their boots, no words, and best of all, no tears—especially her own.

She wiped the perspiration from her forehead and hoped she

wouldn't have any more nightmares. Her heart was still beating fast. She told herself several times to calm down.

Suddenly, Medrano saw Sergeant Acosta walking across the front of the barracks to his office. She crammed her fingers into her mouth, so she would not scream. For a second, she was back in her nightmare. She reasoned that of course he was there. It was his turn to pull night duty.

The sergeants took turns. They had to make sure the fireguards were doing their jobs. She closed her eyes and tried to make her mind go blank. It was not an easy task, but she was determined to do it to make full use of the measly shreds of sleep available. She told herself over and over again that she would be asleep in a few seconds. Finally, she fell asleep.

"Rise and shine!"

Medrano unglued her eyes. Hadn't it been just a few hours ago when she had glued them shut? Why did she feel she never had enough sleep? Her nightmare came back to her. Had she awaken in the middle of the night to see Sergeant Acosta walking to his office, or had that been another dream?

"Rise and shine, people! Get those Army asses up!"

Medrano jumped out of bed and started making her bunk. She always made it before getting dressed since she didn't want to get her uniform dirty. Making a bunk was harder than most civies thought. She had to make sure that the sheets folded nicely in the corners, making "hospital corners." The green bedspread also had to be tucked in the corner. She learned that if she got under the bunk, through the wires that kept the mattress in place, and pulled the bedspread and sheets tightly toward the middle of the mattress, quarters would bounce off the bunk. That was the trick. Any bunch-ups and the bedspread would sag.

She moved from under the bunk and got dressed. Her spirits rose when she realized it was Sunday.

"You sure the sergeant can't prevent us from going to church, Peck?"

"Of course I'm sure, Med," Peck said. "The sergeants can't friggin prevent us from going to church. In fact, they can't even prevent us by punishing us for something. They have to friggin let us go."

"Great! I can hardly believe it!" Medrano exclaimed as she sprinkled an extra helping of baby powder in her shirt. Church was an activity over which the sergeants had no control. She put another generous helping of powder in her in her underwear. "What a day!"

After she put her hair in a bun, Medrano grabbed a broom and started sweeping. Every row had someone in charge of sweeping the floors. She had been chosen to sweep the floors of fourth squad. It was on of the toughest jobs because the sergeants were so picky about the floors. A speck of dirt would send them into a frenzy. When she got to the end of the row, she squinted to see if she had missed anything. She had not, and she smiled at herself knowing that at least she did one thing right in the Army.

I don't know how you have the patience to sweep this darn floor," Peck said. "They expect it to be friggin perfect."

Medrano sighed. "Yes they do."

"They can take a friggin leap as far as I'm concerned."

Medrano figured out what was wrong with the scenario.

"You are acting awfully strange today. You're not swearing. Are you feeling okay?" She touched Peck's forehead.

"I'm feeling fine," she said, slapping Medrano's hand away. "It's just that today is Sunday. I take a break from swearing on Sundays."

"Why?"

"God."

"I thought you didn't believe in God, Peck."

"I like to believe in the idea."

"Idea? Idea of what?"

"The idea that there's some sense out there somewhere even though with what I've seen in life...." Peck's eyes turned sad and glassy.

"What have you seen...."

"See you later, Med."

As Peck strode away, Medrano wondered about her. Imagine thinking of God as an idea? What caused Peck's sadness?

After putting away the boom, Medrano doubletimed it to formation for breakfast. She ate quickly only to find that the soldiers going to the Catholic church had already been marched there. She had to go with the Protestants. To Medrano's surprise, all the Protestants were crowded into one church. As Medrano entered the church, she hoped that the minister would not turn out to be strange. She did not know what kind of a minister she would get. He could be a regular preacher like her cousin's minister, or he could be from some strange religion that worshipped cabbages. In the Army, she didn't know what to expect. All the soldiers sat down without making a single noise. Peck sat next to her.

Medrano looked around. She got the distinct feeling she was at a funeral. Nobody talked. They just looked at each other with fear in their eyes. She thought about when these same soldiers had been so boisterous at the airport. Some childish spirit had been robbed from them. Could it be possible that they were having as hard a time as she?

As the minister went to the pulpit, she braced herself. He seemed normal to her. Probably not one who kneeled down to cabbages.

"Hi, I'm Reverend Johnston. In case you're wondering, I'm a Baptist minister; but don't let that scare you if you're not Baptist. Remember, we're all here to worship God. Now, the first thing I'd like you to do for me is not to look so formal. Relax. This is the Lord's house, and he wants you to be comfortable in it. No, God isn't a drill sergeant waiting to punish you. God knows this too, so stop thinking you're being monitored. No captain or sergeant is allowed to punish you in here, so please relax."

She heard sighs of relief all around her. It was not every day she witnessed a miracle.

As she walked out of the church, the sergeants appeared from out of nowhere to take them back to the barracks. It was time to head back to rough waters.

As they arrived at the barracks, Medrano wondered what great thing the sergeants had in store for them. García ran up to her as she walked in the double doors.

"Guess what we get to do today?" García asked with sparkling eyes.

"Kill subversive soldiers?"

"Be serious, Medrano."

"How about kill drill sergeants. I like that idea."

García chuckled. "Free day, free day."

Medrano's eyes widened. "What do you mean free day?"

"We don't have to practice marching or anything. We get to stay in the barracks and do what we want."

"Are you serious? Who told you this?"

"My squad leader. You see, I got back from church before you did. She explained that on Sundays we do very little; but even so, we still have to watch ourselves from getting into trouble. I mean, we just can't walk out of here. We have to stay inside."

"Wow! That's good enough for me, but why are they giving us this break?"

García considered the question. "The sergeants need a day off, and so do we!"

"They keep getting more human by the minute."

They walked to their respective bunks. Medrano was having a difficult time deciding what to do. It had been such a long time since she had a choice. She looked for Peck, but she was nowhere to be found. Then she saw García polishing her boots with two other females. Grabbing her boots and polishing kit, Medrano went over and plopped herself on the floor next to García.

"I wish I had my Monopoly set right now," said Dekan. She brusquely combed through her short, blonde hair with a pocket comb before starting to shine her boots.

"That would be fun," said García.

"I never play Monopoly," Medrano stated.

"Why?" asked Dekan putting away her comb.

"I'm not good at it."

"You don't do something unless you're good at it, do you?" asked Medrano looked over at some of the soldiers who were trying to get discharged. Some of them had been trying since the first day they arrived at basic. The Army was not going to allow them to break their contracts just like that, but the possibility remained. It would be so easy to give up, thought Medrano.

"But what if you just like doing it?" asked Dekan.

"How can I enjoy doing something I'm bad at?"

"You expect a lot of yourself, don't you?" García asked.

"I don't think I expect enough."

Peck suddenly appeared and plopped down next to them.

"Where were you, Peck? I didn't see you when I first got back," Medrano said.

"I was in the latrine washing some clothes."

"Don't you have them sent out to be washed like the rest of us?" García asked.

"Yes, I do, but a good source told me not to send the dressy T-shirts I bought at the PX. They might get stolen."

The red T-shirt Medrano had bought with Fort Jackson stamped on the front came to her mind. She slept in it, and would hate to have it stolen. It was the only piece of colorful clothing the Army allowed her to have.

"I'm not sending out those T-shirts anymore," stated Dekan, "It's bad enough that we can't have civie clothes here, and but if they steal our colorful shirts...."

"I refuse to sleep in those ugly Army green ones!" exclaimed García.

"I wish I could sleep in my nightgown," said Medrano.

"What for?" retorted Dekan. "No man can get in the sack with you here."

Medrano shot her an irritated look. "Nightgowns are not only for sex!"

"Medrano doesn't screw around," said García.

"Shit, Medrano, you still a virgin?" asked Dekan, surprised.

"That's my business," said Medrano defensively.

"Not everyone fucks around," shot Peck.

"You a virgin too, Peck?" asked Dekan.

"Maybe," Peck said, throwing Dekan such a cold glance that it stopped her from asking more questions.

"All I know," said Dekan, "is that when I get home I'm telling my boyfriend Sammy 'up down, up down, down And don't you get up until I tell you!'"

Everyone laughed, including Peck who was rolling her eyes.

"Is that all you think about, Dekan? Sex?" asked Peck.

"What else is there to think about?"

"Passing basic for one," stated Medrano.

"Basic?" retorted Dekan. "Who gives a fuck about basic?"

"I do," said García. "I want to get the heck out of here."

"You can say that again!" exclaimed Medrano.

They talked about the week and all they had learned, from marching to making bunks. All agreed they hated getting up at 4 A.M. The first chance they had, they would sleep in past 10:00 a.m.

It had been a perfect day for Medrano. That night she rested in her bunk, relishing it. She also was excited by the fact that one week was almost completed. Officially, Sunday was the first day of the week; but for Medrano the week began on a Monday. Six weeks to go! thought Medrano. With that, she dropped into a peaceful sleep, full of happy dreams.

Second Week

The light splashed on Medrano's face, waking her from a deep sleep. Her eyes burned and could not focus. All she could see were dark spots.

"Rise and shine, Medrano," a voice above her said.

"Doggonit! Stop shining your stupid flashlight in my face," Medrano said.

"Time for KP, sucker. You get to clean the mess-hall for good ole Uncle Sam," the fireguard said as she walked away.

Medrano stayed in her bunk for a while. In the Army it was hard to figure out what to expect next. She had no idea what KP (kitchen police) would entail. She checked her watch. It was 3:00 a.m., 0300 hours, and she had to be in the mess-hall by 3:30. She jumped out of her bunk, made it, and quickly got dressed. She checked around to see who else was stuck with KP. She saw Dekan and Willet getting dressed. After checking all her buttons, she started doubletiming it.

"Aren't you going to wait for us?" snapped Willet.

"I don't want to be late." She reached the double doors and ran out.

The crisp air hit her when she stepped outside. It was so quiet. It was so lonely. She could almost imagine that she was the only person alive. Medrano was all by herself. It felt remarkable.

She reached the mess-hall. It felt kind of funny being able to just run inside instead of waiting outside at attention.

"You on KP, slick?" Medrano quickly looked at his lapel and saw that he was a PFC, private first class. She smiled, congratulating herself. She had been able to identify his rank. He was a private like Medrano but with some stripes.

"Yes, PFC."

"Then you're mine for today. Get something to eat with the rest of the bunion-heads. You've got ten minutes. After you finish, I'll tell you what to do."

"Yes, PFC." So far so good, Medrano thought.

She took a tray and was served powdered eggs by a nervous private. She sat down with other soldiers also working KP and put a big spoonful of the eggs in her mouth, took a bite out of a stale biscuit, and washed it down with milk. Then she saw Dekan and Willet running in.

"You on KP, soldiers?" Medrano could hear the PFC tapping a spoon on the counter.

"Yes, PFC," Dekan and Willet said in unison. Their voices cracked a little.

"So glad you could make it. Would you like me to roll the red carpet out for you?" Everybody at the table laughed except Medrano. "Both of you just got on my shit list. You fuck up in any way, and you'll be getting an Article 15. Is that clear?"

"Yes, PFC."

He turned to the table. "Grub is over. The troops will be coming any minute."

Everybody jumped up at the same time and took their trays to the washroom. Medrano couldn't stop thinking about that Article 15. The sergeants constantly threatened them with it. She prayed that she would never get one. It would mean less pay and a criminal record for life. She could deal with the lower pay but could not imagine herself being branded for life. She imagined herself being in front of a prospective employer.

"What's this?" he'd say, looking at her application. "You expect me to hire a convicted criminal."

"Sir, let me explain," she would say with her mouth zigzagging with nervousness. "I was in the Army, and I was given a criminal record for being late to KP duty."

"A likely story. Find yourself a sucker who'll hire you."

That would be the beginning and end of her career. She would end up a bag lady like the ones she heard about in front of the White House.

"You serve the syrup, slick." A voice woke her from her daydream. It was just the PFC.

"Yes, PFC."

Medrano walked to the serving line where the syrup was located. She got the white box with individual envelopes of syrup.

"Slick, don't let anyone have more than one syrup; or you'll be in deep shit."

"Yes, PFC."

"Try not to screw it up, Medrano," sneered Willet who was standing in front of the potatoes with a large spoon in hand and looking as if she was going to lick the world.

"Take care of your own job, okay?!" Medrano exclaimed.

Male soldiers started coming in. The cooks and privates took their positions in the serving line. The PFC got on Medrano's left and served waffles.

Soldier after soldier walked in. Medrano did not pay attention to any of them. She handed each a syrup without so much as looking up until someone grabbed a second syrup from her hand. Medrano's mouth gaped open for half a second. Then she saw Willet's smirk.

"Put that syrup back!" Medrano heard herself yell.

Everybody close by stared at Medrano. She hadn't realized that she had said it so loud. She could feel her face heat up. It turned candy-apple red. She did not know if she was more embarrassed or angry. The soldier giggled and gave her back the syrup.

"You're not a woos, slick," said the PFC chuckling.

"I would hope not, PFC," said Medrano.

After the last soldier left the mess-hall, Medrano got two paper towels from the PFC. She dampened one of them and soaped it. The soap smelled like lemon, and Medrano put a drop in back of her ears. It was not hard for her to imagine that it was perfume.

She and Dekan started on the tables. Medrano swirled the soapy towel across them and then dried them with the other towel. She fervently scrubbed, making sure they were perfect.

"You're taking too long," moaned Willet.

"I want to make sure they look good," Medrano said, continuing to clean the tables.

"It takes you that long to...."

"How long it takes me is my business," Medrano stated, glaring at Willet.

"You're slowing everyone down."

"I am not!"

"Hey, bunion-head," the PFC said, looking straight at Willet, "what the hell are you doing just standing there."

Willet turned bright pink. "I was telling Medrano that she's slowing everyone down, PFC."

The PFC grabbed her collar and pointed to his own with the other hand. "Do you have this insignia on your collar?"

"No, PFC."

"So who the hell told you you could do my job, huh, slick?"

"I was trying to help, PFC."

"Help who? It seems to me that she's the one working, and you're the one standing there yapping away trying to tell people what to do. You should've been an officer, bunion-head. Now, go get a mop and start mopping, and I don't want to hear any shit from you."

"Yes, PFC."

Willet and the PFC left at the same time. Medrano did not look up from the tables for half an hour. She did not want anyone to see her tiny smile. She wanted to gloat.

By the time Medrano had finished a row of tables, the paper towels were tearing and had dark spots.

"Hey, Dekan, are your paper towels in rags?"

"Yes."

"Let's go get some more."

"I wouldn't want to bother the PFC."

"I know where the supply closet is. He got us these towels from there."

"I wouldn't want to get in trouble. Maybe we should ask the PFC for them."

"We're not going to get in trouble for getting a couple of towels." Medrano walked away. Dekan trailed after her. She entered the supply closet while Dekan stayed at the door. Medrano walked straight to the towels and grabbed some.

"Private, what the hell do you think you're doing marching into my office?!"

Medrano's eyes quivered, and her mouth was dry from the lack of saliva. She hadn't seen the sergeant sitting at a desk in the corner. When she watched the PFC take supplies from it, she had assumed the office had been a supply room. She should have known better than to ass-u-me!

"This is my damned office! And you think you can waltz in here whenever you feel like it? Get out, get out!" Medrano did not need to be screamed at again. She made a mad dash for the door. Since she didn't see Dekan, she figured that her reluctant partner had left the scene of the crime a long time ago.

Medrano did not stop running until she was in the latrine. She ran into one of the stalls and vomited. Then she laughed until tears rolled down her face.

After fifteen minutes she dried her eyes and splashed cold water on her face. She breathed deeply, put on a smile, and walked out of the latrine to face her fears. No one was waiting for her. She found Dekan cutting some pies at the serving table.

"Where did you run to, Dekan?"

Dekans voice quivered. "I ran into the food room. The PFC walked in and told me to cut the pies for lunch." Her green eyes were wet like a puppy's.

"Did the PFC know about the office thing?"

"He didn't say anything."

"Don't look so scared, Dekan. I'm the one who's in trouble. He didn't even see you."

The PFC came in with the sergeant from the office. They were discussing the knives they were carrying. Medrano gnawed on her lip.

The sergeant noticed Medrano and looked straight at her. "That soldier over there walked into my office as if she owned it!"

The PFC turned in Medrano's and Dekan's direction. "Who was it? Was it you, bunion-head," he said, looking directly at Dekan.

Medrano and Dekan silently stared back at them. As Medrano was about to speak, the sergeant handed the PFC a knife and walked off. After inspecting the knife, the PFC left also.

"They didn't punish us, Medrano."

Medrano nodded. "I'm sorry about your getting blamed for it. I was about to tell him it was me when they left."

"Don't worry about it. We're off the hook."

Medrano took a towel from her pocket. "Here."

Dekan stared at it, hesitantly.

"Might as well take it. We sure sweated for them."

Dekan slowly took the towel.

Medrano put her hands in her pocket. "I guess we don't have much need for towels at the moment. It's almost lunchtime."

Dekan's eyes brightened up. "Yeah, and I have to finish cutting the pies."

"I'll help you."

"You can take the brownies out of the wrappers and put them on the trays so that they're ready to serve."

"Okay," said Medrano starting to unwrap the brownies. "I love brownies."

"My boyfriend Sammy loves them too. They're so good."

"Let's gobble down," Medrano said. She knelt down, pretending to get more packages of brownies from the cabinet, and put a whole brownie in her mouth. Dekan chuckled and did the same thing.

"What's so funny?" said Willet, popping in from nowhere. Dekan almost swallowed her brownie whole.

"Nothing," stated Medrano.

"We're here to work not to monkey around."

"I'm getting sick and tired of you, Willet. How we do our work is none of your business!" exclaimed Medrano.

"Are you standing around again, soldier?" asked the PFC, magically appearing. "I'll give you something to do." He walked away and Willet followed him with a big scowl on her face.

"She's a wicked witch," Dekan said.

"She's a big bully," Medrano said, putting another brownie in her mouth."

Dekan giggled and started cutting the pies. Medrano finished with the brownies and then helped Dekan with the pies.

Lunchtime came, and the cooks and KP soldiers took their places to serve. To Medrano's relief, she and Dekan were not moved from the dessert line.

Sergeant Grimes' platoon came in first, and Medrano could not help wincing when she saw him. He stood close to Medrano and Dekan, glaring at everyone. Medrano's skin turned clammy.

"You're not going to have dessert are you, fatty?" he asked one of his soldiers.

Medrano almost choked.

"No, sergeant."

Medrano looked at her. She did not seem overweight at all. Medrano was certain she was bigger.

"Put that extra bread back," he told the next person in line. "You already have a butt the size of Texas." His eyes first fixed on her behind and then the rest of her. Medrano was certain his eyes lingered on her breasts.

Sergeant Grimes went on and on, bullying his soldiers then preventing them from taking dessert or taking much food. Sergeant

Washington and Sergeant Acosta came in and watched everything.

"You putting all your soldiers on diets?" asked Sergeant Acosta, with a smirk on his lips.

"They need to be lean and trim in order to do those pushups. Besides, I don't need fat slobs in my Army," Sergeant Grimes said, hiking up his pants.

Medrano thought that his blue eyes turned red. The devil himself, she thought. As his last soldier left, he took a glass of water and walked cockily away.

Sergeant Acosta and Washington looked at each other, smiling and shaking their heads.

"He makes me nervous," whispered Dekan.

Medrano looked over to Willet who was serving the green beans. This was some place to be with power-hungry, kooky people.

The day finally ended. Medrano had expected KP to be much more hectic, but for the most part the PFC had left them alone. He only got on their backs when he saw them doing nothing. So between meals Medrano occupied her day by cleaning everything again and again. She used the same rag, even if it was falling apart. She would not dare go back to the sergeant's office or even ask the PFC for another rag. She was relieved that she didn't have to cook anything. Only the cooks had that job.

Medrano was on her bunk with a big smile on her face when Dekan walked over.

"Hey, Dekan, we survived."

"Want something to munch on?"

Medrano's eyes grew wide, and she looked around. "Food in the barracks? You're a brave soul."

Dekan took out some potato chips and handed them to Medrano. "Here."

"Where did you get these?"

"The storage room."

"You're kidding!"

"I got some fruit too if you want any."

"Dekan, Dekan, Dekan, this is too funny!"

Medrano saw Rogers coming toward her. She quickly stuffed the potato chips in her pocket.

"Medrano, you're on fireguard duty tonight. You're up at nine."

"What do you mean I have fireguard duty? I was on KP all day. I've been up since 0300 hours this morning."

"Do you think I give a shit," she said, walking away.

"If you ask me, she couldn't give a shit even if she tried. Some people don't care about anybody but themselves. It's hard to care when you've got a corkscrew stuck up your ass," Peck said bitterly. She had just returned from the latrine. Water was dripping from her hair onto her uniform as if she hadn't bothered to dry it with a towel.

"It stinks," Medrano said pulling out the potato chips.

"I've got to do that shit tonight too. At nine," Peck said with distant eyes.

"That's my time."

"Where'd you get the chips, anyway?"

"KP," Dekan said proudly.

"Do you peel potatoes and do shit like that?"

Medrano took a bite from a huge potato chip. "Nope. Actually, it wasn't that bad."

Dekan got up. "I'd better go."

After she left, Medrano went to the latrine and took a shower. Afterward she looked for Peck.

"I think it's time to report downstairs, Peck."

Peck looked at her watch. "Shit."

They grabbed their flashlights and doubletimed it downstairs. They reported to Sergeant Acosta who was in a horrible mood. He obviously was not pleased that he would have to stay up all night. He gave them each a helmet. They went back to the barracks and informed everybody it was fifteen minutes until lights out.

All the females started putting their things away, and wrapping up what they were doing. This was not like a huge slumber party where everyone was dying to stay up all night talking. Sleep was a commodity few ever achieved. At 2100 hours no one complained when Medrano turned off the lights.

"Fuck," said Peck.

Medrano smiled. "Wish I was asleep too."

"I hate this. Being on my damn feet all day and then having to walk these barracks all night."

"Tell you what, Peck. You can guard the double doors, and I'll walk the barracks."

"You sure you don't mind?"

"No, of course not. If I minded, I wouldn't have offered."

Medrano walked away. She was relieved that Peck did not want to walk the barracks. Medrano hated doing nothing. Standing there guarding the doors would drive her insane. She would much rather be walking around. Occasionally she would go to the back by the latrines and sit on the floor to rest from all that walking. If she got caught, she would be in serious trouble; but she knew that if she listened well enough, she would hear when somebody came in through the doors.

As she walked around the barracks, she noticed how sound asleep the soldiers were in their bunks. Before basic she heard that in the military there would be homosexuals jumping into one's bunk if one wasn't careful. Medrano rolled her eyes and wondered why people put each other in boxes.

Medrano guessed that there were some gay soldiers in her platoon; but because of the military's stance against them, they kept quiet about their sexuality. Medrano wished some of the heterosexual soldiers keep quiet about their sex lives. So far Medrano had heard more about positions, orgasms, and vibrators than she had her whole life. At first it was interesting; but now because of overkill, it was annoying. Leading the pack of sex maniacs was Dekan who talked about her edible underwear back home and Sammy's big one.

"He's got the big chorizo," Dekan had said. When Medrano looked at her strangely, she stated, "I know a little Spanish."

"Then you'd know that a chorizo is something to eat not...."

"That's why I said his big chorizo." Dekan let out a big laugh.

Medrano felt stupid for having walked right into that one. "So why hadn't you told me you knew Spanish?"

"I only know how to say a few words."

"What w...."

"Chile," Dekan said proudly. "And I can even use it in a sentence, 'Sammy has a huge chile.'"

Medrano rolled her eyes. "What other words do you know?"

"Cochar."

"Do you know any words that don't have to do with sex?"

"Pinchi, cabrón."

"Okay, stop! Someday I'll teach you some nice words."

Dekan's eyes turned mischievous. "Cochar is a nice word."

As Medrano walked farther in the barracks, she didn't want to think of silly conversations anymore. Her mind wandered. Her former existence seemed like a dream to her. Had she ever really lived in New Mexico? Had she actually witnessed the most incredible skies in the desert? Those awesome skies where rainbows would splatter their colors. Now she rarely had the time, strength or inclination to peer up at the heavens. It won't always be this way, she kept telling herself. One day, basic training will also seem like a mere dream.

"Psst, Med," whispered Peck as Medrano passed her.

"What's up?"

"How come you live in your head so much?"

"What?" asked Medrano.

"You get this glassy-eyed look a lot," she said gently rubbing her forehead.

Without thinking, Medrano walked next to her. There was something different about Peck tonight. Something vulnerable for a change. There was still some spice in her words; but she spoke in a very sad way, as if she too was in another world.

"It's the way I survive all of this," Medrano said, staring at her, trying figure what was different about her.

"You think too much."

"Not that old story again," said Medrano, rolling her eyes.

"You like to go into the past a lot, don't you?"

"You don't?" asked Medrano.

"Nope."

"Why not?"

Peck gulped. "Tell me Med, what do you do when your mind wanders to a place you don't want to think about?"

"Self-flagellation—I'm good at that."

"Well, I'm not. As far as I'm concerned, my life starts right here," stated Peck.

"But your life didn't start right here. It started a long time ago."

"Look, Med, this is my reality. I'll make of it what I fucking want."

"Don't get huffy now. Sorry."

Peck sat down, and Medrano joined her. "You'd be huffy too if it was your birthday." Medrano saw Peck swallow hard. "Forget I said that, Med."

"Your birthday! Why didn't you say so?"

"Just drop it."

"How old are you?" Medrano asked.

"I'm twenty."

"It must be horrible to have to celebrate your birthday in this place."

"Sucks." She looked so sad that Medrano wanted to hug her, but she didn't. There was still something about Peck that told her to keep a distance.

"I know." She did not know what else to say.

"You don't understand. Birthdays in general suck."

This caught Medrano by surprise. "You don't like birthdays?"

"Not usually."

"Why not?"

"They're the day you were born," stated Peck. Medrano stared at her.

"As I said before, this is where I begin living," Peck said, taking out her smart book, "and this is my birthday present."

Medrano chuckled. "Some birthday present. I'd rather have a Porsche."

"I've had one of those. No big deal."

Medrano thought she was kidding until she saw the steadiness in her gaze. "You've had a Porsche?"

"Why do you always ask questions I've already answered," Peck said, and Medrano smiled. This was more like the flippant Peck she knew.

"Where in the world did you get enough money, so young, to get a Porsche?"

"My parents."

"Your parents?" asked Medrano.

"My parents gave me a Porsche for my fifteenth birthday."

The double doors opened and Sergeant Acosta walked in. Medrano's and Peck's mouths flew open. They froze. By the time they finally realized what had happened and stood up, the sergeant walked in his office. He had ignored them completely.

"Think we're in trouble, Peck?"

"He would've already screamed at us if we were in trouble, but you never know."

"I'll walk around the barracks."

As Medrano walked away, a thousand and two negative thoughts splashed together.

What if she got an Article 15?

What if she got on the sergeant's shit list?

What if she had to scrub the bathroom with a toothbrush?

What if with all the physical punishment she was left infertile and could no longer have children?

Better yet, what if her children grew up to join the Army were assigned the same sergeant, and got on his shit list by association? They would end up scrubbing toilets and not be able to give her grandchildren.

WHAT IF?

WHAT IF?

WHAT IF?

Her mind was overloading now. Then she started laughing silently at the ridiculous scenarios she made up. "Med, it's time to go to bed," Peck whispered. Medrano checked her watch and sure enough it was 11:00, 2300 hours on the dot. "Wonderful."

As she walked to her bunk, she kept telling herself everything would be okay. As soon as her head hit her pillow, she fell asleep.

Asleep.

Asleep.

She entered her other world the—world hidden deep inside her head. She was on KP again, and the PFC was screaming at her for walking into the sergeant's office. She finally found the courage to look up to him. But when she did, it wasn't the PFC at all. It was Sergeant Acosta, and he was pointing an M-16 straight at her. Straight at her!

Water sprung through every pore of her body. She put her hands over her eyes and realized she was no longer in her dream. She was awake. She took her hands from her eyes and was in the barracks—not on KP. Her hands were slippery, and her mouth was dry. Even though she wanted to drink some water pretty badly, she didn't dare get up. She wasn't sure what she was afraid of, but fear prevented her standing. After about an hour, she finally fell asleep. Her mouth was as dry as a desert.

Medrano did not know why she checked her watch. This was something she automatically did every morning when the fireguard woke the barracks up. It was 0400 hours. What did she expect? They always woke them up at that time.

Before Medrano could consider a couple more minutes in bed, she sprang up. She immediately regretted it. She felt nauseous and light-headed. A deep, throbbing ache pulsed through her head. She knew what it was. She had not gotten enough sleep. In fact, judging by how she felt, her body didn't think it had gotten any sleep at all.

She went with her day as usual. It was almost routine by now. Medrano cleaned. Medrano got in formation. Medrano ate that "delicious" Army grub. Medrano gave every single Hollywood starlet competition with her very own exercise regimen, designed especially for her by the military. However, one totally unexpected thing did happen this day. She was issued her M-16.

She was issued her nightmare.

She knew the day would come, but she did not expect it so soon. In reality, she did not want the day to arrived. She held the gun and felt the reality of it. It was no longer something she saw in the movies. It was no longer locked within her nightmares.

"What a gun," said one of the soldiers.

Sergeant Acosta stared at her. "What the hell did you call this, slick?"

The soldier lowered his eyes in confusion. "Uh, uh...."

"Third platoon, this is not a gun. Guns are to play with. This is a weapon." Everyone stared at him with awe. "Next time someone calls this a gun, you'll get your ass smoked."

"When will we begin firing this weapon, Sergeant Acosta?" asked Rogers.

This woman can kiss butt, thought Medrano.

"As soon as you rock heads learn a couple of things. First, never let your weapon out of sight even for a minute."

"Even...."

"Yes, you piss with it. You sleep with it. Know where your weapon is at all times. If you have a buddy with you, you may ask your buddy to take care of it while you go to the latrine; but you must sleep on top of it. You rock heads remember that in a war this is your salvation your hope for survival—you lose it, and the enemy has power over you. Furthermore, anyone letting go of their weapon for a minute will have hell to pay. I'll take it apart, give pieces of it to all the sergeants, and you'll have to retrieve them from each one of them. You'll have to pay the fiddler each time."

Everyone stood quiet and stared at each other. Medrano could tell that they were all imagining the punishment they would receive from each sergeant if something like that happened. The punishment from Sergeant Grimes alone would be enough to kill them.

Sergeant Acosta marched them to a room where they joined the other female platoons. Each soldier was given a booklet on the M-16. Medrano opened the manual and read that the maximum effective range was 460 meters. That might impress her if she knew anything about gu...oops, she meant weapons, she thought.

The sergeant giving the lecture told them they would be disassembling the rifle. Medrano could hardly believe her ears. She would be taking it apart. She was assigned a buddy, Peck, who was sitting to the right of her. There was only one towel to disassemble the weapon. The Army sure was cheap, she thought.

They started taking the weapon apart as the sergeant talked them through it.

"Peck, Medrano, why are you taking both weapons apart," whispered García, who was sitting two chairs down from her.

"What do you mean, why?"

"You and your buddy are supposed to take only one apart."

"I think we're in deep shit," Peck said. "I guess that's why there's only one towel."

Medrano shook her head in disbelief. "I wish they'd make everything clear."

"What the hell do we do?" asked Peck.

"I can't put it back together since I don't know how, so let's act as if nothing's wrong."

"I guess that's all we can do."

They kept disassembling as the speaker continued. Every once in a while, Medrano conjured up enough nerve to look sideways at the sergeants to make sure they were not looking at her or her buddy. To her relief, some were almost falling asleep during the demonstration. Others were busy talking. They weren't paying attention to the trainees.

They finished disassembling and started re-assembling. Medrano could smell her sweat overpowering the baby powder. When they finished, a tiny smile crept across Medrano's face. They left the room to turn in their weapon to the supply soldier. They were not allowed to take them to the barracks. The "don't lose sight of your weapon" rule would be in the field.

When Medrano gave the supply soldier her weapon, a breath was released throughout her whole body. It felt like a breeze flowed inside of her, locking the pores of sweat.

She was still smiling when she walked into the barracks. Suddenly her smile disappeared.

"Holy shit," gasped a voice behind Medrano.

Everything was in an upheaval. The trash cans were tipped over, and trash was on the floor. There was white stuff that looked like whipped cream all over the mirrors where the soldiers used to inspect their uniforms. The bunks were undone, literally undone—not just unmade. Mattresses were on the floor, and bunk parts were all over the place.

"Shit, what did those fuckers do this time?" Medrano recognized Peck's voice behind her. Peck walked in.

"I can't believe it. They fucked up the place. I guess we're not cleaning to their fucking satisfaction," Peck said.

Medrano was speechless. She looked around, trying to make sense of everything.

"Earth to Med, Earth to Med."

"Shut up, Peck."

"Snap the fuck out of it."

"Shut up!"

"I was just trying to help."

"I don't need your bossy help!"

"Chill out."

"I'll chill out when I feel like it." Medrano walked away, leaving Peck with her mouth open. She did not want to go to her bunk, so she went to the bathroom. She walked straight into a stall and started laughing hysterically without making a sound. She didn't know why she was laughing—it was all so tragic.

When she finally settled down, she calmly walked to her bunk and started putting it together. Rogers came by and started helping her.

"Can't even make a bunk right," she told Medrano.

Medrano glanced at Roger's bunk and noticed it was intact. So the sergeants had not destroyed her bunk. That made sense, since Rogers was an apple polisher. Meanwhile, Medrano's anger began to rise in her throat.

"My five-year-old could've done a better job," Rogers muttered under her breath.

"Really?" Medrano's fury shook inside of her. "Don't help me if you're going to insult me."

"All I meant...."

"I would make my stupid bunk right if someone would tell me which side the U.S. goes on," Medrano said pointing at the large U.S. letters on the cover. "One sergeant tells me one thing, and the other tells me something else."

"I'll ask Sergeant Acosta about it next time I see him, okay?" They had finished making the bunk.

"Okay."

"Grab a broom and start...." Rogers stopped at mid sentence when she saw Medrano's cold stare. "Never mind."

Rogers left. Medrano stared after Rogers with her mind racing. How dare she think Medrano was going to start sweeping just because Rogers ordered her. How dare Rogers think this U.S.—cover problem could be solved just like that. Medrano knew darn well that the "U.S." thing was just bad luck. If Rogers asked the sergeant about it, the other sergeant would think it was wrong. It was just her misfortune that she got a bedspread with an insignia on it. Who was she kidding anyway? Even if she had gotten one without writing, the sergeants would still tear her bed apart. She had been put in that category. The category of a loser. However, she decided she shouldn't feel so bad. Most of the soldiers' bunks were unmade, except those belonging to people like Rogers. Medrano figured she won in the long run, since she didn't want to be anything like Rogers.

"You still in a bad mood?" Peck asked from her bunk.

"Yes."

Peck nodded her head and went back to making her bunk. Medrano was grateful she had understood the message. She did not want to speak to anybody. She thought about the strangeness of the concept of feeling alone in a barracks full of people. Medrano took a quarter out of her wallet and threw it on the bed. It bounced as always.

"They destroyed your bunk too, huh," said García, who had walked up to Medrano's bunk.

"They are such jerks."

As much as Medrano liked García, she wished she would leave.

"García. I need to speak to you!" A voice across the barracks screamed.

"I'll talk to you later, Medrano," said García as she left.

Medrano's prayers had been answered. She smiled as much as she could manage, a small one. She grabbed the quarter from the bunk and put it back in her wallet. Soldiers began running out of the barracks. She glanced at her watch. Shoot, it was lunchtime. Forget being alone. Medrano started doubletiming it. Food might be just the thing to lift her spirits.

After waiting in a long line, she sat down to eat. Her intestines were making noises. She was hungrier than she thought.

"Everybody out. We've got a new bunch of soldiers coming in, and we need you out," said a PFC.

"But we haven't eaten," said a female next to Medrano.

"Do I look as if I give a shit? Get out! We've got a lot of soldiers to feed!"

Medrano stood up, still not quite believing what was happening. She saw other soldiers gobbling down their food as they were taking their trays to the dumpster. She started doing the same. Starving was not on her list of things to experience. She was hogging down a brownie when she put up her tray. At the barracks her fellow soldiers were complaining.

"I'm starving, and they throw us the hell out!" said someone.

"That's the fucking Army for you," said Peck.

"I thought that by law they had to feed you."

"They have to fucking give us food, that doesn't mean we have to eat it."

"Is that why they bothered to serve us and then threw us out?" said someone.

"You've got it."

"What a waste of food."

What lunacy, Medrano thought as her stomach grumbled loudly.

In fifteen minutes it was time for marching practice. Today they would be drilled on marching with their M-16s.

"Medrano, what the hell kind of marching is that? Get with it."

"Yes, Sergeant Acosta." Medrano tried to concentrate, but she was not coordinated. "

"Medrano, down!"

Angry tears trailed slowly down her face as she got in the pushup position. Sergeant Acosta looked at her with disdain. "Those crocodile tears don't do a thing for me. Give me ten, soldier!"

He did not understand. Medrano was not crying because she was being punished. She was crying because she could not march. She felt stupid and awkward. Maybe the other side of the world would be forever unavailable for her. Maybe she was destined to rot on her side.

Medrano felt water hit her. It took her some time to realize it was not her tears and sweat. It was rainwater.

"Okay, soldiers, get inside. You just lucked out."

Everybody gave a yell of happiness and doubletimed it.

"Soldiers to the front," said Sergeant Acosta, who had just walked into the barracks with Sergeant Washington and Sergeant Grimes.

"Sergeant Grimes is going to show you how to properly clean up the barracks. After this, third platoon, I never want to see the barracks look as they did this morning."

Sergeant Grimes began giving them tips. He suggested they put a a strip of masking tape on the floor to line up their boots, so that they would be uniform. He talked about putting on their boots at the doors to avoid scuffing the floor. He went on and on; and Medrano listened intently, thinking how impossible all this was. When Sergeant Grimes finished, they went to chow.

By this time Medrano's insides had stopped grumbling. She ignored her hunger pains. Medrano sat at the table and picked at her food. She took a few mouthfuls and then stood up to leave. Rogers and the other soldiers sitting at her same table stared at her, puzzled. They were gobbling down their food, barely taking breaths between bites.

Medrano put up her tray and doubletimed it back to the barracks. She didn't bother to look around to see if sergeants or officers were there.

As she approached the barracks, it started raining again. She sat on the barracks' steps and let the rain fall down softly on her. She loved the rain. When she was a child, other kids would complain when it rained because they could not go out and play. Not her. The rain had been a gift from God in the dry desert.

She began singing in her head the little song she sang as a child:

Que llueva,

Que llueva,

La virgen de la cueva.

It was a little tune that was supposed to bring about rain, and she would sing it when she was lonely.

Medrano walked up the stairs to the barracks thinking how beautiful the rain was. She took a shower, received nothing during mail call, and climbed into her bunk to sleep.

"Goodnight, Med," Peck whispered.

"Goodnight, Peck."

The lights went out. Medrano did not want to go to sleep. She was sure she would have nightmares. Am I going to make it? This question kept flashing through her mind. It was quiet in the barracks, but her thoughts were noisy. Vignettes of her life appeared. As a little girl she watched T.V. and wished for a comfortable house like the ones on her favorite shows. Parents on television never seemed to have to gather pennies to buy milk. Another scene flashed. School books wide open, Medrano was studying the same material over and over again to make sure she knew everything for a test. She relived her peers' surprise when she had enlisted. The most popular student sneered. That face had haunted her all summer until she left for Fort Jackson in August. Next, she envisioned the film her brother shot of Europe suddenly bursting into flames.

She needed to subdue her mind by talking to someone, but who? Who could she talk to? Peck? Be serious. García? She was way over there. God? Why not talk to God?

Please help me not fail.

Please help me not fail.

As Medrano was saying her litany, a vision of the desert flashed through her mind. No, this wasn't a dream. It was one of the moments she carried with her in her special memory book. Her mind took her back to Sunland Park where a whirlwind of sand pranced through the desert. She had seen this happen many times in her hometown. Sand swirled everywhere, making it impossible to see; Medrano's eyes would tear up from the grains of sand. Then it would rain. The rain doused the whirlwind and settled the sand on the ground:

Que llueva,

Que llueva,

La virgen de la cueva.

Medrano fell into a deep sleep.

In the morning she felt better. She had had no nightmares and felt rested. An unexplainable peace filled her even though there was a throbbing in her ankle. She walked on her ankle, so she knew it was not broken. It did not feel sprained. It did feel as if a vein had broken, and blood was spurting inside of her. She could feel the pulse of the blood. It was a certain kind of freshness. A strange kind of pain.

Medrano went to Rogers, who told her she needed to go on sick call. After they ate, Medrano and a group of other soldiers marched to waiting buses. The buses took them to another set of barracks. They walked to one of the barracks and got in line. Medrano did not know what was supposed to happen. In the Army it was better to shut up and figure out what was happening later.

"Name?" a soldier asked Medrano when she reached the front of the line.

"Medrano, Eliza."

"Social Security?"

Medrano gave him her Social Security number and ran off. In a few seconds he returned with a folder. He handed her the folder, and Medrano followed other soldiers with folders. She took a quick peek inside and saw her records.

The soldiers walked to another barracks where other recruits were already sitting in rows next to each other. The soldiers sat down in empty chairs. As each recruit walked in to see the doctor, her chair was filled by the soldier next to her. Everyone was waiting their turn and moved as a chair vacated.

Medrano noticed a note on the wall which said, "If you're well enough to talk, you don't belong on sick call." Apparently, there were those who had not bothered to read it since they were busily chatting away. A stern nurse walked into the waiting room.

"What did I say about talking? Do all of you know how to read? I'm tired of this. Next time I'm sending you back to your drill sergeants and let them deal with you. Either shut up, or study your smart books."

She went back to the examining rooms. It was quiet for a few moments. Soon soldiers began yapping again, this time in whispers. Medrano wondered why they would take chances like that. She stared straight ahead and didn't mumble a single word. A soldier sat next to Medrano.

"This place sucks, huh?" the soldier asked her.

Medrano turned her head to tell her it was not a good idea to talk. At that very moment the door opened, and the ferocious nurse walked out and looked straight at them.

"You," she said pointing at Medrano, "and you," she pointed at the soldier next to Medrano, "over here." Medrano and the soldier went to her. She grabbed their records.

"Why were you talking?"

"We...," Medrano started to say.

"Never mind, I don't care," she said. She wrote something in their folders that they had to take to their sergeants. It proved they were on sick call. She handed the folders back to them. "Scram!"

The soldier who had spoken to Medrano looked at the nurse with disdain and walked out. The nurse turned and went to the back rooms. Medrano stared at her folder, not knowing what to do. The note said, "This soldier did not get in to see the doctor because she talked too much." She was in serious trouble. The sergeant would smoke her until the cows came home. He would smoke her until.... She did not want to think about it.

Medrano pushed through the door where the doctor was. He was writing on something. The nurse was not in sight.

"Sir, you've got to let me see you. My foot is killing me."

"Wait your turn, soldier."

"Sir, the nurse told me to leave."

"Why, slick?"

Medrano handed him the file. "Sir, I wasn't talk...."

"It says you were," he said dismissing her.

"Sir, she was the one talking to me. As I turned to tell her to quiet down, the nurse opened the door and...sir, I'm really hurting."

He looked at her intently. "Okay, I must be getting soft in my old age," he said, crossing out what was on the sheet in the folder. "Wait your turn."

"Thank you, sir," Medrano said as she walked out the door.

Call her a whimpering, groveling, poor excuse for a human being, but she had convinced him to cross out that awful note. And he was going to examine her. Life was not so bad. She smiled to herself and took the last seat. Someone had already taken hers. She would have to wait about half an hour longer, but somehow it didn't matter.

When she finally got in to see the doctor, a smile kept forming.

"You have tendonitis, soldier."

Medrano could hardly believe her ears. There was actually a name for her malady.

"I'm going to have a semi-cast put on your foot. You'll be put on profile."

"Profile, sir?"

"Yes, you won't be able to do any exercises for a couple of days. Come back in four days, and we'll take the cast off."

"Yes, sir."

He pointed to where she should go to get the cast placed on her foot, and she walked over there. She had wanted to ask him more about the tendonitis, but she knew better. Don't ask, just keep going.

A male soldier put the semi-cast on her very quickly. He did not say a word to her, so she did not say a word to him.

As she was walking out of the clinic, she heard the doctor screaming. "Who do you think I am? Your doctor? Asking all those fool questions! We've got a lot of soldiers to see and you're tongue keeps wagging...." Medrano did not hear the rest. She stepped outside into the sunshine.

On the bus she kept fingering the sheet of paper attached to her Army jacket. It was her profile, and it said she could not exercise for four days no pushups for four whole days. It was too good to be true. She looked through the window and noticed tiny raindrops on the glass. God had not forgotten about her.

When she got to the barracks, she gave the sergeant the note.

"What's this about your talking too much?" Sergeant Washington asked Medrano.

He read the note that was crossed out. How would she get out of this one? Medrano took a deep breath and decided on a strategy.

"The nurse, she kept saying along with the sign on the wall," she was breathless since she was talking so fast, no talking was allowed. I tried to tell this female to shut up, but then the captain understood this and treated me anyway."

Medrano almost laughed at the puzzled look on the sergeant's face. "Never mind...OK, Medrano."

Back at her bunk Medrano smiled broadly. Her devious plot had worked. She had so confused him that he had not asked her to clarify anything. She was thankful for television. She had seen one of her favorite characters do something like this on a show.

"Where have you fucking been?" asked Peck from the bottom of her bunk where she was lying down.

Peacetime: Spirit of the Eagle

"Sick call. I'm on profile."

"For how long?"

"Four days."

"Bitch. How lucky can you get?"

Soldiers started running out, and Medrano realized it was lunchtime. She suddenly felt very hungry.

In the mess mess-hall before she could get in the chow line, Sergeant Grimes walked up to Medrano. She started to perspire.

"Why the hell are you wearing your damn cap inside, soldier?"

Medrano's hand went to her head, and she grabbed her cap. She could not believe she had forgotten to take it off. It must have been the excitement of the day.

"Stupid. You'll never make it through basic because you're too stupid. Go outside and...." He saw the profile and grabbed it. "Take a look at this pussy wimp thing! Poor little princess can't do pushups for four days! After those four days, your ass is mine, soldier," he said as he walked off.

Medrano released her breath. She thought she had been saved by her tendonitis. But what would she do when her profile was over? She stopped herself from going into a frenzy. Moment by moment—that's how she would handle basic.

Third Week

I t was a bright, sunny day. Medrano could feel the sun rays bore into her as her platoon sat on the hard, wooden benches. They were waiting for their turns at the rifle range. As Sergeant Acosta called out letters alphabetically, the soldiers would stand up and wait their turn. Since Medrano's name started with an "M," she still had quite a wait. She re-read a letter from her sister. It was an "everyone is fine" letter. She enjoyed reading it even though nothing new was happening with her family. She was lucky, she thought, that there were no tragedies. She looked up from her letter and saw a billboard about the M-16. It said that if the M-16 was not well greased inside, it would explode.

She thought back to when she was in the formation area outside the barracks. She had picked up her M-16 and cleaned it. She had greased it but then had cleaned off the grease. Had the sergeant said something about the grease? There was so much to take in every day.

Medrano shot up from her seat and ran to her gear. She took some grease, opened her M-16, and globbed grease inside until it was dripping. She wanted to make sure it was not going to explode in her face.

After Medrano finished greasing her weapon, she went back to her place to wait. They were not allowed to speak as they waited. A few soldiers were reading their smart books; most of them were daydreaming. Medrano, having already read her sister's letter, started daydreaming too. She thought of how relieved that she was no longer on profile. It seemed odd to her that she was relieved, but somehow she was. During the four days she had been on profile, she hadn't been smoked nor had she done any exercises. Instead, she had to do light cleanup. It had been heavenly except that she realized she was falling behind the other soldiers. At this rate, she would never learn to do good pushups. She asked Peck what would happen if she couldn't do good pushups. Peck promptly informed her she would be recycled.

"Recycled?" Medrano asked.

"Yes, recycled."

"Like soda cans?" Medrano asked cynically.

"Fuck, Medrano," Peck said. "We're probably crushed worse than soda cans already."

"What is this recycling business?"

"Those shitheads make you go to another battalion, to another platoon to the point where you messed up. Say you don't fire well, you don't qualify, then you go to another platoon that's barely started to use their M-16s."

"That means you're in basic longer!"

"Yep."

"That's scary," Medrano said.

Peck stared at her. "Fear is a cowardly emotion," she said, striding away.

Medrano shook her head and brought herself back to the present. The "Ms" had been called. She stood and waited. When it was finally her turn, the sergeant handed her some rounds for the magazine, a device she had to put into the M-16. Earlier in the day they had been taught how to handle the M-16. They were to point down range at all times, even when they moved backwards. This way they wouldn't accidently shoot anybody. The sergeant giving the class told them a story about a soldier who had turned and accidently pointed the barrel of an M-16 at a sergeant's stomach.

"If it had gone off, that sergeant would've been ground beef," Sergeant Washington said.

"Is that a bad thing?" Peck whispered.

Medrano chuckled when remembering Peck. Before climbing down into the square foxhole, she made sure her military-issued, green earplugs were in right. The foxhole was almost up to her chest when she stood on sandbags. She tried to remember everything she was taught, but it all seemed jumbled together. She stared straight in front of her at the target. It was a piece of paper shaped somewhat like a bottle. Medrano felt strange as she put her breasts against the foxhole. She remembered Grimes' vulgar words a couple of minutes earlier to one of his soldiers who hadn't realized she had to stand closer to the side of the foxhole.

"You let your boyfriends put their hands all over your tits, but you won't put them up against the damn foxhole?"

Then he smoked her until she dropped to the ground.

"Don't lie down! That ain't no man!" he said, snarling.

Medrano put the butt of the M-16 against her shoulder, as instructed earlier and started to shoot. Empty rounds spat out. She was careful not to touch them since she remembered they were so hot they could burn a hole in her skin. It felt strange to be shooting. She never had fired a gun in her life, never had pulled a trigger.

Funny, she thought, some of her neighbors in the barrio were doing the same thing pulling the trigger and for what? They were protecting their territory, and she was protecting United States' territory.

The sergeants started screaming for them to stop. Their time was up. Medrano got out of the foxhole, picked up her M-16, and walked to where the sergeants were checking the magazines to make sure there weren't any rounds left inside. As she was walking, she noticed soldiers dropping plastic apparatuses into a box.

"What are those?" Medrano asked a female in front of her.

"For safety."

"For safety?"

"Yeah. For when you shoot."

A small, gnawing pain struck the right side of Medrano's stomach.

"Where did you get it?"

"It was left next to the foxhole by the soldier before me."

Whoever had been there before her had not left the safety apparatus. Medrano's hands went to her face.

Her face was still there.

Thank goodness. A vivid vision of her mama came to her. Mi mamá estará rezando, she thought, and she could actually see her mama praying. Every day her mama would shut herself in her bedroom and spend an hour praying. She would take her prayer book into her room where the colorful pictures of saints covered the walls. When Medrano was a little girl, she asked her mama what she was praying for.

"Are you praying for a new car, new furniture, or a new house?"

"I'm praying that God keeps us safe," she had stated.

"Safe?"

"Si."

What Medrano remembered most about this daily ritual was her mama's appearance after prayer. She always came out of her bedroom serene and calm. It was almost as if Medrano could see God's touch on her. Even when her mama disciplined her for doing something wrong, Medrano felt gentleness. She felt love.

On the morning that Medrano had left for Fort Jackson, the day her life had changed, she woke to the quiet sounds of her parents who were always up at the first light of dawn. Their muffled voices had seemed like a lullaby, but she had needed to get up and face her new reality. After her shower her mama had said a prayer for her, and a calm had spread through her like water hitting a paper towel. Her decision didn't seem so bad then.

Medrano felt sprinkles of water land on her face. The rain brought her out of the peaceful memory. She was once again on the range.

The sergeant finished checking the magazines. He made sure the soldiers had not smuggled rounds off the range. Afterward he marched the platoon to an area where the mess-hall people were serving chow outside. The chow was in paper bags.

"Great, no fucking C-rations today," Medrano heard Peck whisper behind her.

In actuality Medrano didn't mind C-rations. They tasted different from anything Medrano had ever eaten.

She thought of her mama's frijoles and chilito. There were three kids in her family, and her mama never had problems with them not eating.

The concept of children passing up a meal was strange to Medrano. Food was life. It was a privilege and not a luxury. She guessed that when it was taken for granted, kids didn't want it. Her mama had never mentioned all the starving children in the world. That was not why Medrano ate her peas when she was a child. It was the look in her mama's and papa's eyes. They worked so hard for those frijoles on the table.

It was that same look that prevented Medrano or the rest of her siblings from going wild when they went to a store.

"I want this."

"You have to buy me this or else...."

Those sentences were in her household. Her parents, especially her mama, did not believe in spoiled children. Whatever her mama and papa could afford to give them, that was what they received, and they were lucky to have what they could get.

As Medrano received her bag of food, she thought, how lucky to have something to eat. C-rations, sandwiches...whatever.

In the barracks that night, Medrano noticed the empty bunk across from Peck's bunk was now occupied. The new female was a young Latina. Medrano was sure she was Latina. She was petite, but her obvious confidence made her look taller. Her eyes were introspective as if preoccupied with a million deep thoughts, and her mouth was a straight line as if too busy to smile.

"Medrano," Dekan called, walking toward Medrano.

"What's up?"

"Let's shine our boots," she said as she sat next to Medrano's bunk with her shining kit. Medrano took out her own kit.

"That M-16 is something, no?" asked García.

"It's something all right," said Medrano.

"I can't wait to fire it again."

"I can."

"Who is that new female?" asked Dekan.

"I have no idea."

They were talking about the day. All of a sudden Sergeant Washington started mail call. Medrano and Dekan put their kits away and ran to the front where Medrano received a letter from Linda, her sister.

"You're from Sunland Park?" asked someone behind her as soon as mail call was over.

Medrano turned around and was face-to-face with the new soldier who was eyeing Medrano's envelope.

"You know where that is?" asked a surprised Medrano.

"Yes, I was born in El Paso and was raised there until I was eleven."

Medrano became defensive. She hated telling people where she was from. Sunland Park was a working-class community, and too many people made fun of the working class. How many times had she heard jokes from certain El Pasoans about Sunland Park before they knew she was from there?

She remembered one particularly painful incident. She had been hired at a fast-food restaurant. A manager was training her and three other employees in physical appearance.

"Make sure you are properly combed and that your uniforms are pressed. You don't want to look like you just came from Sunland Park," he had said.

"But I am from Sunland Park," Medrano had blurted out.

There was an awkward silence. The manager at least had the decency to blush before changing the subject.

The new female must have taken note of Medrano's defensiveness. She immediately said, "I loved it there. I used to go visit my aunt Quiróz González all the time. Do you know her?"

Medrano's body became less tense. "No, I don't think I do. Maybe my mama knows her."

The soldier looked at Medrano's name on her shirt.

"Your mama wouldn't happen to be Belia Medrano, would she?"

Medrano's eyes widened. "Yes!"

The female also seemed excited. "Then you must be Eliza!"

"How did...."

"My parents used to take me to San Martín de Porras church on Sundays, and you always were there with your familia."

Medrano looked at her name—Canela. She made her mind go back in time until she mentally scanned the faces in church.

"Adela. Is that your name?"

"Yes! What a coincidence!" Canela exclaimed.

"It's a small world, huh?"

"Very small," said Canela.

"I remember that all of a sudden you and your family no longer went to church."

"We moved to Los Angeles."

"How's your mama and papa, Adela?" asked Medrano.

Canela's excitement vanished. A veil of sadness enveloped her. "They're gone, Eliza."

It was as if a fighter had landed a solid punch in Medrano's chest. If she remembered correctly, the Canelas were a joyous family always surrounded by people who wanted to partake in their positiveness. How could Adela's parents be gone? Dead? Tears desperately wanted to run out of Medrano's eyes.

"I'm sorry, Adela. I didn't know."

"It was a freak accident," Canela said rapidly, as if she wanted to get it out and not talk about it again. "How's your mama and papa?"

"They're doing well."

"Does your mamacita still make that wonderful menudo on Sundays?"

"Still does."

"M-m-m. How are your brother and sister?"

Medrano thought with sadness how Adela had been an only child. Who had been there to share her pain? Who had been there to understand?

"They're fine."

Canela smiled weakly. "One of these days I'd like to go back to Sunland Park to visit. Unfortunately, my tia no longer lives there."

"Come stay with us. My mama would love to have you visit, Adela."

"I'd really like that."

Medrano smiled. "There's not a lot of people who dream of visiting Sunland Park."

"It's a neat community."

"I wish everyone thought so," Medrano said, thinking of the fast-food manager.

"Don't you ever feel Eliza, that you need to justify living in Sunland Park. There are jerks out there who think being poor monetarily means being poor in spirit. They are the same idiots who think money buys you class. That it buys you soul—as if it's a sin not to have a bunch of money. As if money makes you a better person. What a bunch of crock!"

"There's this yellow journalist in Las Cruces who did a story on Sunland Park. She wrote that no one spoke English there, that everyone was illiterate, that all the houses were one room shacks and that the only food people ate were beans."

"So much for truth in the media."

"A lot of people in Sunland are middle class; and many students from there, such as me, graduate in the top ten percent of their class. That stupid, yellow journalist never reported that."

"No, of course it wasn't reported. It didn't fulfill a stereotype."

Talking about this to someone who understood and shared her anger allowed Medrano's pent-up frustrations out. Without having to say it, Medrano was sure Canela knew what it was like to fight with the beasts of "I'm not good enough." Subliminal messages delivered through the beast of stereotypical media depictions greatly upset her.

"I wish there was more respect in this world," said Medrano.

"What a dream."

"You're new here," cut in Dekan, who had just walked over.

"Yes."

"Were you recycled?" Dekan asked.

"No. I was in second platoon."

"With Sergeant Grimes?!" Medrano and Dekan exclaimed in unison.

"He transferred me here."

"Why?" asked Medrano.

"We didn't get along. Grimes hated me, and I hated his racist, SEX-ist guts!"

"He's a real jerk!" exclaimed Medrano.

"You're lucky he's not your drill sergeant," Canela stated scornfully.

"He makes me uncomfortable," said Dekan.

Canela became extremely animated. "That's because he's thinking of ways to jump your bones as he's looking at you."

"I knew it. I knew it." Dekan's voice was shrill. "He porks some of those soldiers, doesn't he?"

"Sexual harassment?" asked Medrano.

Dekan's eyes slanted. "Has he tried anything with you?"

"No! He knows better than to try anything with me!"

"But he tried things with the others, didn't he?" Dekan asked.

"I don't have proof—the others don't say anything about it—but I'm pretty sure it's happening. I think they're scared."

"Lights out in fifteen minutes," warned one of the fireguards.

Medrano got in her bunk. Her head was still swimming with all that had been discussed among them.

The lights went out, and Medrano's eyes were flooded with tears as she thought about Canela's parents. Then she thought about grimy Grimes taking advantage of his position. Medrano could still see his eyes pawing the females, and a disgusted tremor passed through her. It was a long time before sleep overtook her.

This is weird, Medrano thought.

She was in a lecture room full of females from all the platoons. A mirror and make-up tray sat in front of each female. They were being taught how to apply make-up by a beauty consultant.

"What the hell is wrong with this Army?" whispered Peck.

She was sitting in front of Medrano. "First they tell you that you can't wear make-up with your fatigues, and then they have a class on make-up. Does that make sense? This is fucked up."

"Do I hear someone yapping over there?" asked Sergeant Acosta.

Peck immediately shut her mouth, and Medrano started applying blush the way the beauty consultant instructed.

Next came eye shadow. She chose a shade of brown for her lids. With a disposable mascara wand, she applied black mascara to her eyelashes.

When the session was over, they were taken back to their barracks to take off the make-up. As they stood in front of the mirrors ready to scrub it off, they looked at their faces.

"This is fucking ridiculous," said Peck. "They tell us we can't wear it. Then we have a class for it. Then they make us take the shit off."

Medrano smiled at Peck. She was surprised to see how different Peck looked with a bit of make-up behind her ugly black-rimmed, Army glasses.

"You should be a model, Peck," said Medrano.

Peck guffawed. "Model? Be serious!"

"You have one of those faces you can make look like anything. Anybody. Look at how that make-up changed you."

"I wish I could look like a model," Dekan said.

"Why?" asked Canela.

"Isn't it obvious?" asked Dekan.

"No."

"Because that's the epitome of beauty."

"Who said?" asked Canela.

"Magazines, T.V., and...."

"Screw those one-faceted ideas of beauty. Screw those clueless magazines. Screw those stupid commercials that tell you to wear colored contacts to be beautiful. Screw...."

"You've got five minutes!" Rogers yelled. They hurried to remove their make-up.

Faces scrubbed bare, the females marched to the field. They were learning how to adjust the sights on their M-16s. This was called zeroing.

Medrano got into the foxhole and looked at the cardboard target in front of her. She was supposed to shoot at a circle in the middle toward the top. The First Sergeant periodically moved something at the top of Medrano's M-16 to adjust her sights, and then she would shoot. As soon as she got three consecutive shots within the circle, she knew her sights were adjusted.

The weapon felt strange in her hands. She was still getting used to the idea that all she had to do was pull the trigger. Could it be so easy? Killing someone wasn't more difficult? The first few times Medrano fired, none of the holes were in the circle. She tried again, but only one hit in the circle. Medrano kept firing and kept missing the circle. Sometimes she hit two, and sometimes she only hit one.

"Stupid thing," she mumbled.

Soldiers were coming in and out as Medrano kept trying to get those three shots in one little circle. The circle was becoming smaller by the minute. The sergeant announced that there were fifteen minutes left.

"Doggonit," Medrano uttered under her voice.

Then she had an idea. She wasn't too proud of it, but her head was hurting from the loud rifle fire.

"First Sergeant, First Sergeant," she screamed at him.

"You finally finished, slick?"

"Yes, First Sergeant."

"Let me see," he said looking at the circle. "Did you shoot those three holes consecutively?"

"Yes, First Sergeant."

"Alrighty, slick. You can leave."

The First Sergeant walked away, and she jumped out of the foxhole.

Liar, liar, a voice inside of her chanted. She knew they weren't consecutive.

After she gave the sergeant the remaining rounds, it occurred to her that she hadn't zeroed. Her weapon was not in tune with her.

How will I shoot my targets?

What if I don't pass?

What if I'm recycled?

What info, I'll live day-by-day. No, not even that. I'll live moment-by-moment. The next day she didn't have time to worry about zeroing. A new challenge was set for her.

She stood in line looking at the blue sign. It had the name of the course, Victory Lane, and start point. She started for the first obstacle. She had to cross a river on a rope which was hung across the river. The river was not full of water. Instead it was a little stream full of huge, menacing rocks. The rope didn't look too strong, Medrano thought.

Peck came to the rope first. She looked terrified. Her whole body shook and her mouth was pinched tight.

"Keep going, slick. Don't stop," the sergeant told her.

She went slowly, crawling on top of the rope at a snail's pace with her body intertwined with it. Once Peck was farther away, the sergeant signaled Medrano to get on the rope. She did.

It was not as hard as she thought it would be. She kept back her fear and inched her way to the other side of the river. Ahead, Peck stopped often. The sergeant would tell her to keep going. But Peck's pace delayed Medrano.

As she waited, she couldn't hold on to the top of the rope any longer. She fell upside down as her hands gripped the rope. She kept trying to inch forward as she hung underneath. When she found a place where the river wasn't so deep and rocks so large, she let go. Medrano landed on her feet, close to the other side.

"Slick, why'd you let go?"

"Sergeant...."

"No excuses, slick," he said as he turned from her. "Hurry up," he told Peck, who was still on the rope.

Medrano climbed out of the river and went to the next obstacle. It was a wall made of planks of wood. She had to climb over the wall with a rope which came from the top of it. The soldiers in front of her were having a lot of problems.

Then one of the soldiers said, "The hell with this," and ran around the wall. She'll be in trouble, Medrano thought. Then she realized that the sergeants were busy at the first obstacle trying to get soldiers like Peck over the river. Medrano and all the other soldiers ran around the wall.

The next obstacle was a group of ropes held up by wooden stumps. The soldiers had to crawl under the ropes. There were so many soldiers going through that the ground was full of ruts. They had to crawl extremely low. Their backs could not hit the ropes. Medrano waited in line feeling disgusted. Because it had rained, the ground was full of water and mud. Soldiers were wading through it; and the watery mire covered them, filling their noses.

"I'm skipping this shit, too," Willet said and walked off. Medrano was deciding whether to follow Willet when Sergeant Acosta appeared.

"Why the hell isn't your uniform muddy, Willet?" roared Sergeant Acosta.

Willet turned around. "Sergeant, I...I...."

"Get your finicky ass over here, and go through it. You're lucky I'm in a good mood today, bunion-head!"

Medrano enjoyed seeing Willet scurry back like a frightened mouse. Ever since the debacle with her in KP, trying to tell everyone what to do, Medrano secretly wished she would get her comeuppance.

"No, not in that one!" Sergeant Acosta screamed. "Get in the muddiest one!"

Willet scowled as she crawled in. Medrano noticed a smirk on the rest of the soldiers' faces. It seemed no one liked her.

"Hurry up, Peck," Sergeant Washington yelled.

Medrano turned to see Peck trying to climb the wall. She would only get halfway up the rope and then drop to the ground.

"What the hell are you doing, Peck? Playing twinkle toes!"

Medrano saw Peck's face. She looked horrified. What was she scared of? Medrano knew Peck wasn't scared of the sergeants, so why were her eyes bulging?

Medrano's turn came up; and she plopped herself down, ready to scramble under the ropes. She could feel the mud swish over her and scrunched her lips tightly, hoping none would get in her mouth. It was becoming a challenge to keep from vomiting as she felt the dark water dancing on her skin.

When she got through the whole ordeal, her uniform was covered with muck. The hot sun would soon dry it.

After that the obstacles seemed easier. She went through metal tubes, swung on ropes, and walked on logs. Medrano was surprised that she was having such a good time.

She had the most fun on a wooden apparatus with several vertical logs. She climbed up. The other side had a rope she used to climb down. Medrano was already on the ground when she heard Peck's voice.

"I can't get down, Med!"

Medrano looked around to find Peck at the top of the apparatus. Her back was facing Medrano. Peck had made it to the other side of the apparatus with the rope.

"What's wrong, Peck?"

"I...."

"What?"

"I hate heights!" Peck screamed.

"You're scared of heights?"

"I hate heights, and I can't come down. Please help me."

Medrano moved to the other side so she could see Peck's face. Peck was hugging the top log so tightly she was turning purple. Medrano was sure she could see blue veins popping out of her skin. She could feel Peck's fear.

"How can I help?"

"Help me. Help me get me down, Med. Get me down!"

"I can't go up there, or we'll both fall but...."

"Please help me!" Peck screamed.

"First, let's calm down. Shush. Let's calm down."

By that time, one of the soldiers had called Sergeant Acosta.

"What's wrong?" he asked.

Medrano was afraid he would make matters worse if he started screaming at her. She would fall off for certain. It wasn't that high up; but still, falling could do some damage.

"She's scared of heights," Medrano said.

He looked at Peck's trembling body. He nodded.

"Peck, we're going to make it down, okay?"

"Yes, sergeant," she said with a shaky voice.

"You're going to be fine, Peck," he said.

"Yes, sergeant." She did not sound very convinced.

"Now, I'm going to stand here. If you fall, I'll catch you. Put your right hand on the rope."

"I can't."

"Yes, you can. I'll catch you if you fall. Put your hand on the rope."

"What if you don't catch me?"

"I will."

"But...."

"I'll catch you," Sergeant Acosta assured her.

"But...."

"It's not that high of a distance to fall from, Peck."

"I won't crack my skull?"

"No," Sergeant Acosta said.

"You sure?"

"Yes."

Peck looked at the ground, put a shaking hand on the rope and clutched it.

"Good, Peck. Very good," the sergeant said. "Slowly put the other hand on the rope."

She tried to; but each time she would almost touch the rope, she'd pull it back and grab the log.

"C'mon Peck. I know you can do it," he called.

She finally grabbed the rope.

"Muy bien. Now wrap your legs around the rope slowly."

"But...."

"I'll catch you."

She wound her legs tightly around the rope and started to inch down. It seemed as if everyone was holding their breath. Medrano saw that Peck's eyes were shut the entire time she came down.

"Excellent," the sergeant kept saying.

When Peck's feet finally hit the ground, a collective sigh of relief was heard.

"Good job, Peck," he said.

Medrano felt a hand shake her awake. She tried to open her eyes which were heavy with sleep. Her body slowly awakened.

"Rise and shine, Medrano."

Medrano checked her watch. It was 11 P.M. What was that in military time? Who cares, she thought. She hated fireguard duty. It wasn't so bad at 9 o'clock before she went to bed. But when her sleep had to be disrupted, it stunk.

She and the other soldier on duty dressed, reported downstairs, then came back up. As usual, she asked to walk the barracks while the other female guarded the doors. She was thinking about the films her brother had taken of Europe when she walked past Peck's bunk. Her face was horribly contorted, and her skin was as shiny as when they had finished PT this morning. She had such a hard day, thought Medrano, with the fear-of-heights thing. After that incident Peck had stayed away from everyone and had not said a word. All of a sudden Peck started shaking in her sleep and whispering frantically, "Don't, don't, please don't!"

"Peck!"

"Don't."

"Wake up, Peck."

Peck started getting louder. "Don't die. Please don't!"

"Peck, wake up," Medrano said, putting her hand on her shoulder.

"No!" Her hand shot up to Medrano's chest and smashed against it. Medrano fell back onto the floor, her flashlight falling and breaking in big pieces.

Canela woke up and ran to Medrano, who was on the floor trying to catch her breath. Peck stared at her, disoriented. "Are you okay, Medrano?" asked Canela. Medrano nodded.

"What's going on?" asked a soldier.

"Nothing. A flashlight fell to the floor and got busted," said Canela. "Go back to sleep."

"Hold down the noise," said a female who was turning over.

"Why'd you hit her?" asked Canela, looking at Peck.

"I was having a nightmare."

"Do you often hit people in your dreams?"

"Sometimes," Peck said, getting up as if to end the conversation. Peck picked up the pieces of the flashlight off the floor, went to her locker, and took out her flashlight.

"Look, I'm sorry I hit you. Here," she said handing the flashlight to Medrano. She went back to bed and turned her back to Medrano and Canela.

"I need to go splash some water on my face," Medrano said, gasping between every couple of words. Canela helped her up, and they walked to the latrine where Medrano splashed cold water on her face.

"Feel better?" Canela asked.

"Much better."

"Good."

"I can't believe her," Medrano said.

"You mean Peck?"

"She almost kills me, says a barely audible apology, and then turns her back on us."

"She's definitely got problems."

"At least she gave me her flashlight."

Medrano always hated tests. She was waiting in line to do pushups for her PT test. The goal was to do 16 good pushups in two minutes by the end of basic training. That was the requirement for females to pass. All the females were having problems with their pushups. At least I'm not the only one, thought Medrano. Sergeant Acosta kept shaking his head.

When it was Medrano's turn, she barely managed to flex her arms. It was a vast improvement from when she first arrived and almost immediately dropped to the ground.

"You've got a long way to go, slick."

"Yes, sergeant," Medrano said, standing up. She went to stand in the situp line.

Situps were a different story. She could do them all day long. She needed to do 27 within two minutes to pass requirements. When her turn came, she did 35.

Next came the two-mile run. The sergeants told them that running two miles within 22:14 minutes was easy. "You should be able to walk the two miles in that span of time. Just take it easy."

Medrano had to run around the track eight times to equal two miles. By the fourth lap she had to order her legs to keep going. It reached the point she could almost ignore the squeezing in her chest and the quick burst of air she kept taking. She ignored the heaviness of her feet when they hit the black pavement. When she ran two more rounds, the exhausted feeling subsided. She knew she could manage the last two laps. It turned out she came in under 22:14 minutes. She ran it in 20 minutes.

Medrano was glad when they returned to the barracks. "The PT test is over," she silently rejoiced. Before changing into their camouflage uniforms, the sergeants wanted to talk to them in the dayroom.

"A lot of you are far behind when it comes to pushups," said Sergeant Washington.

Medrano's eyes started rolling. She knew something she didn't like was about to be said.

"We're starting a sixth squad on Monday for those who are having problems with upper strength," said Sergeant Acosta. "This sixth squad will have PT two times a day—one in the morning with everyone, and a second at night. We start next week."

Medrano looked at García, and both shook their heads. Sergeant Acosta read the names of those who were going to be in the sixth squad. Medrano didn't blink when her name was called.

"The next thing I wanted to talk about is that the captain inspected the barracks today and congratulated us on being the cleanest," said sergeant Acosta.

Everyone yelled from joy.

"Good going, third platoon," said Sergeant Acosta. "As a reward Sergeant Washington and I have decided we'd let you go with your platoon guide to the PX on Sunday."

This was great but still did not make up for the sixth squad. If Medrano could barely handle PT once a day, how would she survive it twice a day? García, who had also been inducted into the torture squad, kept shaking her head sadly.

"It won't be so bad," said Canela as they walked out of the dayroom.

"What won't?" Medrano asked.

"Sixth squad. Isn't that what you're worried about?"

Mind reading, Medrano thought, always amazed her. The Army was definitely a place to develop certain abilities.

"It'll all be over soon," Medrano mumbled.

Medrano felt someone watching her. She looked toward Peck and saw Peck eyeing her. She seemed to want to say something. Ever since the night Peck hit her, they hadn't spoken. Medrano abruptly averted her eyes and looked at Canela.

"Third week is almost over. Four more weeks and we'll be through, right?" Medrano asked.

"Right."

Standing in formation for the PX, Medrano could feel her wallet yelling, "Let's do some spending!" Sergeant Washington spoke to them before they went to the PX.

"Third platoon, usually candy isn't allowed; but Sergeant Acosta and I want you to buy mouth fresheners, plenty of them like Certs or Lifesavers. Nothing is worse than a funky mouth breathing on us when we're talking to you. Also, get plenty of deodorant and soap. Some of you have a bad case of B.O., and Sergeant Acosta and I have it hard enough without having to suffocate with your funk."

Walker, the platoon guide, marched them to the PX. They waited outside the PX for each squad to go in and come out. They had fifteen minutes. Fourth squad finally went in. As soon as Medrano walked inside, she grabbed a diaper for shining her boots, toothpaste, soap, talcum powder, shampoo, and deodorant. At the checkout she grabbed a box of Lifesavers. She stared at the candy bars longingly. She also stared at PEOPLE magazine. It was against regulations for her to have magazines. What the heck, she thought. At the last minute she bought the magazine and a Hershey candy bar. There were no other soldiers in line anyway. No one had seen. She stuffed the magazine in her camouflage pants and the candy bar in one of her pockets. Then she doubletimed it outside.

When the last soldier came out of the PX, they marched back to the barracks. Sergeant Washington made them stay in formation while he checked the paper bags.

"Willet, didn't I tell you to buy something for your mouth?"

"Yes, sergeant."

"I don't see anything in here," he said pointing at her bag.

"I didn't think I needed mouth fresheners, sergeant."

"You didn't think. Slick, if the Army had wanted you to have a brain to think with, it would've issued you one."

"But...."

"Did I just hear a but? When I tell you to do something, you'd better damn well do it. Is that clear, slick?"

"Yes, sergeant."

"Next time you go to the fucking PX, you'd better have Certs coming out of your ass, or its that same ass I'm going to smoke!"

"Yes, sergeant."

"You're lucky today is Sunday, and I'm in a generous mood."

"Yes, sergeant."

"This is the last time I want to smell your funky breath."

He checked Medrano's bag. When he was done, she finally took a breath. She felt the magazine sticking to her skin, the Hershey bar starting to melt. When she arrived at her bunk, she quickly took out the magazine and chocolate bar and put them in her locker. Peck stared at her, but Medrano ignored her.

"Third Platoon!" yelled Sergeant Washington from the front. "I'm leaving, and I'd better not hear you were doing something wrong! You are not allowed to step out of the barracks. Your ass is mine if you disobey my orders!"

He left. They stared at each other thinking this was a trick. They had never been left alone before. Fifteen minutes passed before they believed it. The females started taking out candy bars and Walkmans from their lockers. Medrano had not been the only one breaking the rules. She thought she was brave until she saw these females with Walkmans. She didn't feel brave enough to go that far. She could get rid of a candy bar quickly, and she could tear the magazine in tiny pieces and flush it. But the Walkman radio was too expensive to have to throw away if it was found.

Medrano looked at her watch. She had two hours before bedtime. Her boots were shiny, and her locker was straightened out. She lay on her bunk reading and munching, but it felt too strange to be on top of her bunk. She hit the floor underneath and immediately felt at home.

A calm thumping on the roof of the barracks made Medrano smile. The falling rain lulled her. Her heart beat to the rhythm. The chatter around her became more and more distant to her. She put her hands together and closed her eyes, feeling the serene presence of God. She felt enveloped in warmth.

"You think God is listening?" Peck asked sarcastically.

She was also on the floor, under her bunk.

"Yes," Medrano said, opening her eyes and leafing through her magazine, pretending to ignore Peck.

"God doesn't listen, Med."

Medrano abruptly closed her magazine. "Why do you say that?"

"He already knows everything. Why should He listen?"

"But...."

"The only thing God does is punish to keep order in the universe. Don't you know that by now? He's not for the weak-hearted. He's for the lionhearted. He is an angry and vengeful God."

"I like to think there is more to God than rules, regulations, and punishment. Much more."

"What more? Love?" sarcastically asked Peck.

"Yes."

"And what else is there to God?"

"I'm still searching, Peck."

"What bullshit," she replied.

Medrano shook her head and picked up her magazine again.

"Maybe you can pray about being in sixth squad?" Peck asked, turning to face Medrano.

"I already have."

"You're worried aren't you?"

"If I am, so what?"

"You worry too...."

Medrano put down her magazine. "Don't even start."

"But..."

"Don't even start because I know the truth," Medrano stated.

"What truth?"

"That you're as scared as the rest of us."

"What the heck are you talking about?" she asked defensively.

"You were scared at the obstacle course, weren't you?"

"Let's not get into that!" Peck exclaimed.

"You're a fake, Peck."

"Don't you ever call me a fake!"

"You've got fears just like any human being."

"Shut the friggin up, Medrano. You don't know what the heck you're talking about."

"Why do you put up a front?"

"Put up a front? So you think you know me so well, Med. You don't know me at all!"

Peck turned away. Medrano thought how true her words were. Who in this world knew the enigma that was Peck?

Medrano looked across and saw Canela sitting on the floor shining her boots. She got up, walked over to her, and sat down.

"Hey, Eliza."

"Adela, are you ever scared?"

"Todo el tiempo."

"Really?"

"Yes, always."

"You don't look scared."

"People deal with fear differently," said Canela.

Medrano looked toward Peck. "Yeah."

"Dealing with fear is part of life. I'm sure that even the soldaderas were scared."

"Who?"

"The soldaderas," Canela said, looking at Medrano's puzzled expression. "They fought during the revolution in Mexico."

"Females in the front lines?"

"You better believe it. You know, Eliza, we come from a long history of bravery. Our men have received more Medals of Honor than any other group."

"Really?"

"Yes. We're a brave people."

"Brave and fearless, huh?" asked Medrano.

"Bravery doesn't necessarily mean fearlessness."

Medrano thought about it for a while. "How good are you at pushups, Adela?"

"In one word—excelente!"

"Must be nice."

"Wait till you hear why I'm so good at them. I got my butt smoked nonstop by Grimes."

"Jerk!"

"It sucked."

"Do you ever feel that you're walking on a tightrope without a net?"

"Eliza, I've already fallen and crashed; but I know how you feel," said Canela.

"In high school I always felt I had to get top grades, so I could get into college. My parents couldn't help me with homework. They don't have much education, and they couldn't afford to help me financially for college. I never had a safety net."

"Your safety net is yourself, Eliza."

Fourth Week

Medrano felt the tiny drops of rain soak through her uniform, giving her a welcome reprieve from the burning sun. She looked to the heavens and smiled. Then she took the diffused grenade and positioned herself behind the line. She stretched her right leg back and balanced on it. She bent her knees, extended her empty left hand in front of herself, and bent her right arm over her shoulder. As she sharply snapped her right hand upward, she put her left hand behind her. The grenade flew over the rope, and she smiled proudly. Her happiness quickly waned when she noticed the hard time Morningstar was having.

Morningstar could not get her grenade over the ropes. She kept trying, but the grenade would not go high enough. Her face was plump with frustration.

"I've been practicing for a stupid hour." Morningstar grumbled. "I need to qualify with these things," she said as she held out the grenade.

"Maybe if you concentrate on the rope itself."

"What?"

"Stare at a point over the rope, and throw it toward there."

Morningstar stared intently over the rope, and threw the grenade."

"It's is no use!" Morningstar exclaimed.

"You really want to make it through basic, don't you?"

"Doesn't everybody?"

"You work harder than all of us put together," Medrano said.

"I have to make it through."

"Why?"

"Because—"

"Yes?" Medrano asked.

Morningstar looked at Medrano long and hard. "I have kids to support."

"I didn't know you were a mother."

"I'm not actually a mother."

"But you said...."

"They are my sister's kids. Her husband left her, and she was having a hard time making ends meet so I...."

"You what?" Medrano asked.

"I volunteered to join the Army and send her my checks."

"Why didn't she...."

"It's hard leaving the reservation."

Medrano thought back to when they were allowed to go to the PX, and everyone got so excited. The only one who rarely went was Morningstar. When she did go, she bought only the basic necessities.

"You're something else, Morningstar."

She eyed Medrano intensely. "Poverty is not fun."

"I know. Believe me, I know."

As far as Medrano was concerned, the only good thing about sixth squad was that at least they didn't have to do PT with weapons. When they had been rounded up for the second PT for the day, Medrano was dreading having to deal with her M-16. It was always part of morning PT. Whenever they did pushups, they dropped the weapon over their hands and proceeded. It was exhausting.

As she entered the barracks after nighttime PT, a group of females ran up to Sergeant Washington who was behind Medrano.

"Sergeant Washington! Sergeant Washington!"

"What?"

"It's Bodine, sergeant!"

"What trouble has Bodine gotten herself into now?"

"She took a whole bottle of pills."

"What?" yelled the sergeant. "She swallowed all of them! Bodine! Get your ass over here!"

Bodine came from the back of the barracks. "Yes, sergeant."

"Did you swallow a bottle of pills?"

"Yes, sergeant," Bodine said calmly.

"You did?"

"Yes, sergeant."

"Why the hell would you do a stupid thing like that?"

"I don't know."

"You don't know?"

"Her daughter, sergeant," said one of the females.

"Her daughter?"

"Her daughter is...."

"What's wrong with your child, Bodine?"

"She's very sick, sergeant," said Bodine as her eyes grew misty.

"That's not a reason to try to kill yourself. Now, get to the hospital. You two," he pointed at two females, "go with her."

They left for the hospital. Medrano headed to her bunk.

"Poor Bodine," said García. "I can't believe she tried to kill herself. Bodine just found out her little girl has cancer."

Medrano's heart beat faster. "What?"

"She has cancer."

"How old is she?"

"Six," García said.

"Medrano, you've just been moved up to fireguard duty at 2100 hours," said Rogers, appearing out of nowhere.

"I have?"

"You're first."

Medrano checked her watch. It was 15 minutes until 9:00. She excused herself from García and ran to the showers. As the water hit her, she let out a flood of tears. Cancer in a six-year-old. How did that happen? Why?

When Medrano turned off the lights, she hoped to walk the barracks. Fortunately, Dekan chose watching the double doors. As

Medrano walked away, Dekan took out her Walkman and put on the earphones.

As Medrano was walking the barracks, she heard an urgent whisper coming from Dekan. "Medrano! Medrano!"

Medrano ran to her. "What?"

"Officers, Medrano. I saw officers through the crack between the two doors. They went to another platoon first."

"You saw them?"

"We're being inspected tonight."

"I'll go and make sure everything's okay," Medrano said. She walked away as Dekan took off her Walkman and hid it behind the trash cans. A few minutes later, she heard some yelling.

"What kind of a poor-ass soldier are you?"

What do I do, wondered Medrano. Two officers were laying into Dekan big time.

"Isn't there supposed to be another soldier on duty!" exclaimed one of the officers.

Medrano doubletimed it to the front. Before she could follow procedure, one of the officers jumped on her.

"Get your ass next to your buddy, soldier!"

Medrano stood next to Dekan who was shaking as if she had just seen a rattlesnake. Dekan had her hand in a salute, and Medrano did the same.

"Do you know what your incompetent buddy did?"

"No, sir," Medrano answered. In her peripheral vision, she noticed the trash can was knocked over.

The officer shoved the Walkman in Medrano's face. "We'd better not find one of these things on you."

"No, sir."

"Didn't you two idiots know these are against regulations? Are you not only ugly but stupid too?"

Dekan's cheek began to twitch almost out of control.

"By the time I get through with the likes of both of you, you won't know which way is up. I'm giving you both Article 15s!"

Medrano was about to ask them why she was getting one if it wasn't her radio.

"Article...," Dekan started to say.

"Did I give you fucking permission to talk?"

Dekan bit her lip.

"Did I?"

"No, sir," Dekan said with a trembling voice.

Medrano decided it would be best to keep her mouth shut.

"You," he said pointing at Medrano, "go check to see that all the soldiers are covered before we inspect the barracks."

Medrano nervously went to every bunk, making sure the females were all covered. After she finished, the officers went to the dayroom. Medrano felt her breathing quicken. She had forgotten to check the dayroom. Sure enough, there was a camouflage jacket lying there.

"What the hell is this?" yelled the officer as he picked it up. "What the hell is this doing here?!"

"Sir, I...."

"Shut up. There's no fucking excuse for this!"

They ordered Medrano to return the jacket. She looked at the name tag, found the soldier, and made her get up and put it in her locker. When the soldier opened her mouth to complain, Medrano gave her an angry glare. She mumbled something, put it away, and went back to bed.

Medrano and the officers went from bunk-to-bunk. Everything was fine until a pair of red underwear was spotted on the floor next to a bed. Then they went to the fire escape. Medrano had never known she was supposed to check this area, her drill sergeants had never mentioned it. They came back with cigarette butts.

"Don't these stupids know it's against regulations to smoke in here?"

Medrano wanted to tell them she didn't smoke but kept her mouth shut. She knew the females found it difficult to wait for permission to go down to smoke in the formation area, so they smoked on the fire escape.

"Article 15s! That's what you two are getting."

Since she was already getting an Article 15 for the Walkman fiasco, Medrano wondered, was she getting another one for the barracks fiasco? When they left, Dekan started pulling her hair.

"We're in real trouble, Medrano."

"Bodine is in real trouble. Not us." But Dekan wasn't listening to Medrano. She was running to the lights and turning them on.

"You worthless jerks! Pieces of Army shit! You got Medrano and me in trouble!"

Females were waking up, rubbing their eyes, and looking puzzled. "We're getting Article 15s because of you!"

Medrano ran to the lights and shut them off.

"Calm down, Dekan. Calm down. We'll be okay."

Their shift was over soon after that. Medrano lay in her bunk. For some reason she wasn't scared about the Article 15s.

In the morning, after making her bunk and getting dressed in record speed, Medrano started sweeping the floor. When she got to Willet's area, she noticed Willet had shoved her bunk into the middle of the aisle. This made it difficult for Medrano to sweep. She had to stop and go around Willet's bunk with the industrial sweeper. Medrano saw Willet slowly combing her hair.

"Willet, would you please put your bunk back; so I can finish sweeping?"

"No," she simply said.

"No?"

"You heard me."

"Listen, Willet. I have a lot to do, so I would appreciate it if you move your bunk back."

"No."

"How dare you say no. Here I am busting my guts to keep the floors clean while all you do is primp. You are not assigned to anything."

"Just sweep around my bunk, okay?" she said smugly.

"Move your stupid bunk, okay?" Medrano said with a menacing

voice.

"Do your job and shut up."

"You...."

"What's going on here?" asked Rogers, walking up to them.

"Willet is making me do twice the work. All she has to do is move her bunk back, so I can finish. It's not like she's busy doing her own chores. She's standing there primping!"

"That is my business. I'm not moving my bunk till I feel like it."

"Medrano, just sweep around her, okay?"

Medrano felt fury sweep over her from inside her stomach. Then it swirled into a boiling mess. With one powerful arm, she shoved the sweeper in front of her. Dirt scattered all over Willet's boots. For a couple of seconds, everyone stood frozen in shock.

"I can't believe you did that!" screamed Willet. "You got my boots dirty."

"Medrano, what the hell did you just do?" asked Rogers.

"What you told me. I was finishing sweeping the crap off the floor."

"I'm reporting you to the sergeant, Medrano," said Rogers.

"Go ahead, Rogers," Medrano said.

"You're going to be in real trouble," stated Rogers.

"What's going on here?" asked Walker. She and Canela were coming out of the latrine.

"Nothing I can't handle," stated Rogers.

"I said what's going on here?"

"She threw crap all over my shoes," said Willet.

"Medrano, did you do that?"

"Yes, I swept dirt over her feet."

"Why?"

"I was in a hurry sweeping, and I nicely asked her to move her bunk back in place, so I could finish the floors. She refused."

"Why'd you refuse to put your bunk back?"

"She can sweep around it," said Willet.

Walker stared at her with fiery eyes. "Put your bunk back right now!"

"But...."

"But my ass! Do it right now!"

"I'm not."

"What the hell is all the commotion?" asked Sergeant Acosta, walking into the barracks, "And what's this bunk doing in the middle of the aisle?"

Willet's mouth opened nervously. "Medrano threw...."

"Is this your bunk, Willet?"

"Sergeant, Medrano...."

"I wasn't asking you about Medrano. I was asking you if this bunk is yours?"

"Yes, sergeant."

"It doesn't belong in the middle of the aisle."

"I was going to put it back, sergeant."

"I don't want to ever see this bunk in the middle of the aisle. Is that clear?"

"Yes, sergeant."

"Put that bunk back immediately, and sweep. Your area is a mess, soldier; and so are your boots."

She made an exasperated noise. "Sergeant, I was saying about Medrano...."

"Did I give you permission to speak?"

"No."

"You are one of the most annoying individuals I've come across. The gas chamber will soon cure you of some of your better-than-thou-ways."

Medrano saw the mocking look in Willet's eyes. Don't do it Willet, she kept thinking. Willet could not help herself and let out a snort.

"What was that, Willet?" asked Sergeant Acosta.

"Nothing, sergeant."

"You're making fun of the gas chamber?"

"No."

Sergeant Acosta smiled. "We'll see who has the last laugh," he said, chuckling as he walked away.

Walker's eyes were still flaming. "You listen to me, you self-serving bitch. When I tell you to do something, you do it. Now, clean up! Medrano, give her royal highness the sweeper!" she exclaimed as she strode away.

Medrano shoved the sweeper at her. Willet looked at Rogers for help, but Rogers walked away without saying a word.

"You don't have to be such a bitch. We're all trying to survive this!" yelled Canela. "C'mon, Medrano, let's leave her alone with her work."

"Bye," Medrano said to Willet as they were walking away.

"Nothing I hate more than a bitch without a cause. It's okay to be a bitch with a cause. It's when one is without a cause that one gets in trouble."

"Adela, what's the gas...."

"Don't ask. You're better off not knowing what the gas chamber is," Canela stated.

"But...."

"It's better to just deal with it when it comes instead of obsessing over it."

"So you're not going to tell me, are you?"

"Nope."

When they reached the formation area, Dekan was ecstatically happy. She called to Medrano as she got in position.

"The sergeant gave me back my Walkman."

"He did?"

"We're not getting Article 15s after all." Medrano smiled. They saw Sergeant Acosta coming toward third platoon and stopped talking.

When they arrived at the mess-hall, Medrano noticed Willet was not there. She was probably still sweeping. As she was about to take a bite of her bread, Medrano saw Bodine coming in dressed with her civilian clothes. Bodine was wearing a pair of blue jeans and a bright red top. Medrano wished she could put on her civilian clothes, even for only a moment.

"She's getting discharged because of her little girl," whispered Canela in between bites.

"Poor Bodine."

Bodine sat at the table next to Medrano. She was about to take a bite from her scrambled egg when Sergeant Grimes walked up to her.

"You want to see a loser?" he screamed around the mess-hall. "Look at this loser!" He pointed at Bodine. "Couldn't make it in the Army, huh?"

Medrano looked at Bodine, who looked exhausted and as if she couldn't muster enough strength to say a word. Medrano wanted to shout that Bodine wasn't getting out because she wasn't able to make it through. She was getting out because her daughter had cancer. Idiot! Grimes had assumed she had pleaded, like others, to be released from the Army. Medrano had already seen some of them leave after managing to convince the military they needed out. This process took quite some time to accomplish, but some succeeded.

"If we look under the word loser in the dictionary, we'd see your picture."

What an original line, thought Medrano as she rolled her eyes. She looked around to see if her sergeants were there, but neither of them were. Deep inside, she wanted to believe that if they had been there, this awful scene would not have occurred.

"Tell him something," whispered Canela.

"I saw you move your fat lips, Canela!" Medrano winced at the way the sergeant said Canela's name. He pronounced it Cain-ela.

"You're just a loser like your friend here," he screamed.

"I just hope you never have a child with cancer and have to be discharged from the service to take care of her, Sergeant Grimes."

His eyes registered shock, and his face turned beet red. Dozens of disgusted eyes bored into him. He quickly regained his composure.

"You're not supposed to be talking in the damn mess-hall, Canela. Pick up your tray and get the hell out. You too," he said, pointing at Medrano.

"Gladly, Sergeant Grimes," said Canela, as she stood up.

Outside the mess-hall, Medrano fervently shook her head.

"Jerk!" Medrano exclaimed.

That day was the first time Medrano didn't find weapons PT so bad. Maybe because she was not concentrating on the exercises at all. At other times she had to force herself to think of other things. But not that day. There were so many things to think about. On other occasions she kept telling herself to take everything minute-by-minute. Now she seemed to do it automatically.

The day to be introduced to the the gas chamber finally arrived. Medrano could not keep her, "don't-think-about-it" stance any longer. She didn't know what upset her more. She was having problems with her M-16; it would often jam. Now she was about to enter what the sergeants kept telling her would be one of the worst experiences in her life. Sergeant Acosta said the gas chamber is a room with CS gas, which is what Mace is.

The sergeants marched them to the chamber. Two squads were to be in the room at all times. They were told they were to put on their gas masks and enter the chamber. Then one squad would be asked to take off their masks while the other squad watched. After a certain period, the first squad would be released from the chamber. The other squad would take off their masks. When a squad exited through the other side of the chamber, they were not to stop walking under any circumstances.

"You vomit or drop anything third platoon, you'll be going back into that chamber from hell. Make sure you hold on to your gas masks. Don't leave them inside, or you're going back to get them!" yelled Sergeant Washington.

"Sergeant Washington, not everyone is scared of the gas chamber," stated Sergeant Acosta.

"Is that true? Who is the bunion-head who doesn't have the sense to be terrified?"

"Private Willet."

"You're not scared, Willet?" asked Sergeant Washington.

Willet's eyes were sneering. She puffed out her chest to twice its size. "No, sergeant."

"We'll see how brave you are. You'll be begging us on your hands and knees to let you out."

"I don't think so, sergeant."

The sergeants didn't say anything. They only laughed. Second platoon, Sergeant Grimes' platoon, was almost done. Medrano wished she could see the soldiers coming out, but the exit door was on the other side. Since Medrano was in fourth squad, she would be the last to enter. She waited nervously.

Finally, her squad's turn came. Medrano slipped on a gas mask which covered her whole head. She thought they looked like aliens with big plastic eyes and a black-nose apparatus in the middle. The mask was suffocating and hot. Medrano tried to beat back a twinge of claustrophobia. Fourth squad entered and stood behind third squad. She saw something that looked like an old-fashioned, wood stove which she figured was the source of the CS gas. Medrano smiled. This was not so bad. She wondered why the sergeants, who had their masks firmly on, were carrying brooms. Third squad was ordered to take off their masks.

Pandemonium broke loose. Soldiers started shaking and jerking with coughs. Could it be that bad, Medrano asked herself. The only one who stood straight as an arrow was Willet. She was toughing it out all right.

One female dropped to the floor and lay spread-eagle with her hands and feet spread apart. Her face was contorted with pain, and her eyes were shut. As Medrano was about to check her to see if she was alive, the female suddenly scrambled up and ran for the exit door. The sergeant blocked the exit with his broom, and she ran back to the spot and plopped herself down into the same position.

Medrano saw another flash going toward the door. It was a second female trying to make it to safety. Again the sergeant's broom stopped her. All this time Willet stood with her chin up as if nothing was paining her.

"I want to hear your general orders," stated Acosta. "All at the same time." He eyed the female on the floor.

Two female soldiers quickly pulled the soldier up from the floor, and third squad recited their general orders.

"Get out of here, third squad, and don't drop your masks!"

They started doubletiming it out. Willet was almost at the door when Sergeant Acosta stood in front of her with his broom.

"Where are you going soldier?"

"I...."

"Get your ass back in. Stand next to fourth squad."

"I...."

"Are you arguing with me? You want me to smoke you in here?"

Medrano saw that Willet was shaking when she walked over to their squad.

"Fourth squad, take off your masks."

As soon as the mask was off, Medrano felt a heaviness on her face. Her nose and mouth burned. Then her skin started feeling red and scorching.

"Damn, double damn, double damn!" Peck kept saying over and over.

Every breath Medrano took was like breathing fire. She tried to stop breathing, but this made matters worse. When she finally inhaled again, she had to take a big whiff. She felt liquid running out of her mouth and nose. Her skin stung more with each passing moment, and everything seemed to be happening in slow motion.

"We're in hell!" Peck said.

Medrano suddenly recalled what she'd learned in biology class. Gas traveled up. She hit the floor. While it still felt as if she was burning, it was more like second-degree burns rather than third-degree ones. She flattened herself to the floor.

"Get up Medrano!" yelled Sergeant Washington.

Medrano begrudgingly stood up. Meanwhile, Willet was kneeling down in front of Sergeant Acosta begging him to let her go. Her tears mixed with snot. Medrano had to do a double take when she saw Willet, since for a few minutes she was unsure it was really her. Sergeant Acosta ignored her and walked up to third squad. Medrano and the other soldiers started reciting their general orders.

"Did I tell you I wanted to hear those orders again?" asked Sergeant Acosta.

Medrano's throat was aching. "No, sergeant."

"What was he he going to ask them to do?"

"Sing Itsy-Bitsy Spider."

Everyone's eyes grew large and stared at him.

"What?" said Peck.

Sergeant Acosta said to sing Itsy-Bitsy Spider," stated Sergeant Washington.

Everyone stood shocked.

Sergeant Acosta lifted his broom. "You can start any time you want. I have all the time in the world."

Medrano started singing. Everyone immediately joined.

"There's one of you not singing, said Sergeant Washington. He glanced at Willet who looked as if she was ready to burst with anguish.

"Sing!" Medrano yelled.

"I can't. I can't."

"Sing!" all the other soldiers ordered.

"Sing!" Peck screamed as she stomped her foot in front of her. The soldiers surrounded Willet, giving her threatening looks. Willet started to sing with a voice so shaky that Medrano wondered if she was going to make it through the whole song.

"Okay, that's enough. Get out of here fourth squad."

Medrano dashed for the door. She was The first one to get there even though she had been the farthest from the exit. As soon as she dashed out, she put on her helmet. She carried it along with the gas mask. She made sure she did not drop anything, since she was not about to make any mistakes to make her return to that horrible place. The sunlight sparkled on her face, and she took the deepest breath of air she had ever taken. Then she saw Sergeant Grimes eyeing her.

"You'd better not stop, or vomit. Keep walking the trail."

Medrano doubletimed it past him and followed the little trail which led to where soldiers were walking in a circle.

"Keep walking," said a drill sergeant from another platoon.

Medrano joined the circle and kept taking deep breaths. It suddenly occurred to her that she must have run out pretty fast. The rest of fourth squad was just joining her.

What took you so long she wanted to ask.

"Isn't it wonderful?" whispered Morningstar as she reached Medrano. She walked beside her.

"I thought we'd never get out," Medrano whispered back.

"Look around you, Medrano."

She looked at the cloudy sky and felt rain drizzle on her face. It felt so good to be alive. It felt so good to breathe.

"It's beautiful out here," said Medrano.

"The Great Spirit is truly great."

"What is the...."

"The Great Mystery."

"I don't know what...."

"God. The Great Spirit is everything, and everything is connected," Morningstar said. Her unclenched hands went over her heart, and then she swung them out.

They were ordered into formation. Back in the barracks, the soldiers started talking as soon as they hit the doors. The only one not talking was Willet. She sat alone on her bunk staring at the wall.

"That was the most horrible thing I've ever experienced," stated Dekan.

"You haven't lived much, have you?" asked Peck as she walked to the latrine.

"How long were we in that horrendous place?" asked Medrano.

"A couple of minutes," replied Canela.

"That can't be!" exclaimed García.

"No way we were in there for only a few minutes," insisted Medrano.

"She's right," said Morningstar. "I timed it."

"Unbelievable!" exclaimed García.

"Those were the longest minutes of my life. Everything was going in slow motion as if it would never end."

"It ended, thank goodness," said Canela, "Just don't forget what the sergeant said. Shower with cold water, or the hot water may re-activate some of the CS gas that penetrated on our skin. Then it's the gas chamber all over again."

The next morning Medrano was certain the CS gas was killing her. She had a stomach ache and vomited in the latrine.

"Are you sure it's not psychosomatic?" asked García. "We were put through a traumatizing situation."

"I don't think it's in my head," said Medrano. "The vomit was pretty real."

It was nerve racking for Medrano. She couldn't decide whether to go on sick call or not. Today would be the day they were qualifying with grenades. If she went on sick call, she would have to qualify at another time, without familiar people surrounding her. Yet, if she was about to throw the grenade and started vomiting, she was likely to kill everyone. With that thought she decided to go on sick call.

As it turned out, her illness had nothing to do with CS gas. She had a mild case of stomach flu.

The next day Medrano was in a room full of male soldiers, waiting to qualify with the grenade. The only other female was outside qualifying. She might as well have been a male, she thought. She was dressed exactly like them. The males talked to each other as Medrano uncomfortably waited her turn. She decided they were as frightened to talk to her as she was to talk to them. Fraternization was against regulations.

One particular instance of the dangers of fraternizing was etched in Medrano's mind. She had been cleaning her weapon with the rest of her platoon when one particular toilet-mouthed, male soldier stared at all the females, made lewd gestures, and yelled, "COME to me baby. COME! I know what all you horny bitches want!" He hadn't noticed Sergeant Acosta walking up behind him with lips as tight as a fully stretched rubber band and a deep furrow on his eyebrows as deep as the Grand Canyon.

"What the hell are you saying to my soldiers, slick?" he growled.

The soldier was so taken by surprise that his face lost all color, and he didn't say a word.

Sergeant Acosta paced in front of him. "Can't you open your fucking mouth? Just a while ago you were saying plenty, slick!"

Sergeant Acosta proceeded to make him do what seemed a million and two squat thrusts and a billion pushups. By he time he finished with the soldier, sweat was swimming down his septic mouth; and he was crying. Medrano almost felt sorry for him. Almost. She still couldn't forget his lewd gestures and insulting tongue. A grenade, like the one she would throw shortly, wouldn't have been bad if it were placed in his mouth.

Medrano stared through large windows at the first soldiers about to throw grenades. The fort was arid and desert-like in this area. Fort Jackson was lush and jungle green. The sand of the grenade range made her think of the segment on Sesame Street where they ask, "What doesn't belong in this picture?"

The bright, almost blinding sand caused a gnawing sensation in Medrano. She could clearly envision the desert from where she came. As her thoughts drifted toward home, explosions ripped the air. Sand bombarded and saturated the entire area. No wonder there wasn't any grass here.

"Get down!" yelled one of the soldiers, "That female is about to throw a grenade."

"You think because she's a female, she can't throw a stupid grenade," yelled Medrano.

"It's a known fact that females aren't as strong as males."

"You don't have to be a body builder to throw a stupid grenade, Einstein!"

The nerve of him, thought Medrano. They had all proven they could throw far enough with a defused grenade, or they would never have been allowed to throw a live one. The explosion from the female's grenade sounded. She had done fine. Several of the male soldiers looked relieved. Medrano's stern look deflated the male soldiers' frail egos; they did not meet her eyes.

Finally, it was Medrano's turn. She wondered if the male soldiers would scrunch down in fear, when she threw a grenade. She walked to her assigned launching grenade position. There were several stations in a row with a sergeant over. When Medrano got to her area, the sergeant told her not to worry about anything. It would be easy. He instructed her to throw the grenade, then hit the ground. But if for any reason she did not throw the grenade far enough, she should jump into a hole behind them and lie down. He would jump on top of her.

"But that's not going to happen," he said smiling. He handed her the grenade. She tried not to think about how this one differed from those she had in practiced. This one was live.

"Slowly take out the pin, but make sure you squeeze the lever down."

Medrano held the lever tightly as she pulled out the pin. No one had to tell her about how important that lever was. As long as she squeezed it down, the grenade would not be activated.

"Are you ready?" he asked.

"Yes, sergeant."

"I'm going to count to five."

"Yes, sergeant."

"Remember, don't get nervous. You'll do fine."

"Yes, sergeant."

He took a deep breath. "One...Two...Three...."

"I can do this, I can do this," Medrano chanted silently. "Four...."

The last number seemed to take forever.

"Five!"

Medrano mustered all the strength in her body, and launched the grenade, and hit the ground. After the explosion, she stopped shaking.

"You did excellent, soldier!" exclaimed the sergeant, "You did better than most of those bunion-head males," he said chuckling.

Later that day at the firing range, Medrano kept congratulating herself on how well she had done on the grenade range. Her M-16 was giving her trouble again. She was getting so frustrated. She just wanted to throw her hands in the air and say, "I give up!"

"What's wrong, Medrano?" asked Sergeant Acosta, "Why aren't you firing at the targets?"

"It's my weapon, sergeant."

"Go see if there's anything wrong with it."

Medrano jumped out of the foxhole and headed for the truck where weapons were checked. She gave her weapon to a PFC and dreaded the outcome.

Your M-16 is fine; it's you who can't shoot soldier, Medrano anticipated hearing.

"Your M-16's bolt is all screwed up, soldier," said the PFC .

Medrano stared at him.

"Did you hear what I said?" he asked.

"Did you say my M-16's bolt is messed up, PFC?"

"Yes."

"Really?"

He chuckled. "No doubt about it whatsoever. Give me a couple of minutes, and I'll replace the bolt."

Moments later she was back in her foxhole shooting, Her M-16 did not jam once. This is what it's like to be shooting with something that works, Medrano thought.

"Did they find something wrong with your weapon, Medrano?" asked Sergeant Acosta.

"Yes, sergeant."

"They did?" His voice sounded completely surprised.

"It was the bolt, sergeant."

"The bolt?"

"Yes, the bolt was damaged, sergeant."

"I'll be damned," he said as he walked away.

Medrano started firing again. She had a lot of catching up to do. Tuesday would be qualification day, and it was already Saturday. Her throat constricted every time she thought about it. She'd only fired a few rounds when it was time to stop.

By the time third platoon arrived at the barracks, it was late. Medrano couldn't believe how little sleep she was getting these days. Ever since they had received their weapons, the days seemed to be getting longer. There were always ranges to go to and classes to take. She had been to a first-aid class that day. As usual, she had trouble paying attention since she had to fight the urge to doze. Other soldiers told her how they slept through classes with their eyes open. Medrano thought it was impossible until she had fallen asleep herself.

"Lights out in half an hour," Walker shouted.

Medrano took a five-minute shower, not bothering to wash her hair. She didn't care that she had not washed her hair in several days. When she returned from the showers, she saw Canela at her bunk, shining her boots. Medrano promptly went to her locker, deposited her shower supplies, and grabbed her boots and shining kit.

"Hi, Eliza," said Canela.

"Hi," Medrano answered plopping herself down beside her.

"Boy, am I tired."

"Me too."

"This stupid Army is making us work like dogs," said Canela.

"Don't they think we need any sleep?"

"At least it's almost over," Canela said. She sang part of their favorite cadence, "Three more weeks and we'll be through."

"This week's not quite over yet, Adela."

"Let's pretend it is."

"I wish I could think like that. I think I'm going to be recycled.

"Why is that?" asked Canela. "

"My M-16. I've been practicing on it not knowing that the bolt was messed up until today."

"Did you get it fixed?"

"Yes, but what good does that do me on this late date? We qualify on Tuesday, and tomorrow is Sunday. The last day I get to practice is Monday."

"Don't lose hope, Medrano. How did you do with the grenade qualification?"

"That I did very well. By the way," Medrano said, looking for Morningstar and not seeing her, "do you know if Morningstar qualified?"

"She fucking got a waver," interrupted Peck, as she passed by the two.

"Waver?"

"Yeah, the fucking sergeant got her waved from grenade qualification. Can you believe that?"

"Can they do that?"

"Apparently they damn well did. And I thought those people had no trouble with anything outdoors."

"Who are those people?" asked Canela.

"Indians."

"And you think every Indian is good at the outdoors?"

"Well...."

Canela's lip was trembling. "How many John Wayne movies have you watched anyway?"

"I don't fucking watch John Wayne movies!"

"You got your stereotypical ideas from somewhere!"

"I...."

"Did you know that Medrano and I are Indian."

"No, you're Mexican," she said matter-of-factly.

"What do you think a Mexican mestizo is? Spanish blood with Indian blood."

"Then I guess you and Medrano should be good at the outdoors too!" Peck exclaimed with a wicked smile. She seemed to enjoy baiting them.

"If all Indians are good outdoors, then I guess all white people are rich, huh?"

"I'm rich," said Peck.

Canela stared at her for a couple of seconds. "Why are you here if you're rich?"

Peck's smile immediately vanished. "Why are you here?" asked Peck defensively.

"Hell, I'm not here by choice. That's for sure."

"What do you mean?"

"I don't think any so-called 'minority' or women should join until the system works better for us."

"Then why did you fucking enlist?"

"The judge told me either I'd join the military or go to jail. You can guess which I picked."

Medrano's and Peck's eyes bugged out.

"You're a criminal?" asked Peck.

"I broke a building's windows. Lots of windows."

Medrano stared intently at Canela. "Why?"

"Why would you do a stupid thing like that?" asked Peck.

"It was the building where my parents worked at."

"So?"

"They knew their damn elevator was faulty, and they didn't fix it."

"And?" asked Peck impatiently.

"My parents died in that elevator."

Medrano winced at the pain in her voice. She was surprised to see some sadness in Peck's face. Could it be that in spite of her hard exterior, she could be a slight bit compassionate?

Peck regained her voice first. "Wouldn't it have been better to sue than to break windows?"

"They declared bankruptcy and then reopened under a different name."

"I'm sorry, Adela," said Medrano.

"The maintenance person kept telling them the elevator was on the blink, but they didn't listen. They'd rather people's lives at risk. Five other people died with my parents," Canela said with pain, anger, and bitterness all rolled into one. "My parents were the most sacred thing to me."

"Shit happens," said Peck as her familiar, hardened look came back.

"But sometimes it shouldn't happen. Not to my father. Not to my mother."

"My mother died too," a bitter Peck said. Canela and Medrano stared at Peck, waiting.

"She did?" Medrano asked tentatively.

Peck glared at her, "Life goes on."

There was a stunned silence. Medrano's eyes filled with tears as she thought of life without her mama.

Medrano broke the silence. "How can you say that? Didn't you love your...."

"No."

"So your life wasn't stereotypically marshmallowy like the Cleavers or the Brady bunch?" asked Canela.

"No," Peck said. She walked away with her back ramrod stiff.

"She can't mean it about her mom," Medrano said.

"I'm sure she doesn't," Canela stated sadly, "Sometimes it's easier to be angry than to cry."

Fifth Week

Was she awake or wasn't she? Medrano was sitting up on her bunk in the middle of the night. She didn't remember doing so. In fact, she didn't feel control of her body at all. Recently it had a mind of its own. She looked toward the front of the barracks and thought she saw Sergeant Washington walking to his office. Was she awake or was she dreaming? Everything looked surreal.

Suddenly Medrano was in the jungle again. This time she wasn't tied up. She was definitely free and carrying an M-16. A huge snake dropped from a tree in front of her. Medrano cocked her weapon and aimed. The snake started laughing. She tried to fire, but the M-16 jammed. "Shoot!" she exclaimed. The snake laughed even harder as saliva dripped from its mouth.

"You can't jam! Your bolt was replaced!" Medrano screamed at her M-16.

The weapon finally fired, but none of the shots hit the snake. "You'll never zero!" exclaimed the snake.

Medrano woke up shaking. She slowly oriented herself. That stupid snake was right, she reflected. I never zeroed. Medrano thought back to when she became so tired on the range she told the first sergeant she had zeroed. In reality the weapon had not been adjusted to her body. Shoot! Stupid snake! She checked her watch. It was 3:30 a.m. She had given up thinking in military time. Thank goodness, she had set her watch for this time before going to bed. She needed to shine her boots. Otherwise the snake might have eaten her. But then, she thought, maybe getting eaten by a snake was better than trying to qualify with a weapon with botched sights, a weapon which had not been zeroed.

Medrano slid out of her bunk, made it, dressed, and headed for the latrine. It would be light enough there to shine her boots. She knew she should have done this on Sunday when she had some free time. But for some reason she couldn't make herself do it. Besides, she was used to getting up at 3:30 a.m. Third platoon usually returned to the barracks late. With Medrano too tired to shine her boots or anything else, she was in the habit of doing things in the morning.

As she started applying black polish on her boots, her thoughts recounted Sunday. The third and second platoons had gone to the P.X. They came back to formation to be checked before returning to their barracks. Sergeant Grimes had his soldiers checked by their platoon guide. The platoon guide patting their bodies like a police officer did when checking a suspect. Grimes looked as if he was enjoying the scenario. He stared intently until cookies and candies started coming out of camouflage jackets and pants. Sergeant Grimes then became furious.

Sergeant Acosta watched the scene, incredulously. He simply checked third platoon's bags. As they went into the barracks, Medrano sensed the soldiers' relief that Sergeant Acosta had not done what Sergeant Grimes did. Medrano subconsciously kept touching the Hershey candy in her pocket. "Poor second platoon," everyone kept saying.

"What cruel punishment does evil Sergeant Grimes have in store for them?"

Later that day when they went out to practice marching, they saw second platoon doing weapons PT.

"That's their punishment," said Walker.

"What do you mean?" asked García.

"That's what Sergeant Grimes did to them for having food."

"That's all?" They were amazed.

"Yes. This is the first time they've had to do weapons PT."

"But we do weapons PT every day!"

It all sounded so unfair; but as the sergeants were fond of telling them, "Deal with it!"

Medrano was trying to "deal with it" at the firing range. Now they had practice runs with moving targets rather than stationary ones. They needed this practice.

"Third platoon, listen closely to what I'm going to say!" Sergeant Acosta yelled while they were in formation outside the range. "I've heard several of you belly-aching about how your sights are screwed up. It doesn't matter. You can still qualify. Aim and fire, third platoon."

It made Medrano feel better that she was not the only one with the zeroing problem.

In the foxhole she tried to remember what Sergeant Acosta said. As targets came up, she missed them. She tried to concentrate. The cardboard figures appeared in different places—some close, some far, and two or more appeared at the same time. She fired, but only a few went down because she had actually hit them. Most would disappear before she fired at them. She became confused and began hesitating on the trigger. I'm going to fail, she kept thinking. I can't hit these stupid things. When she was through, an officer read how everyone did. As suspected, she did horribly. The officer told those who had done poorly that they'd have one more practice.

"I'm going to give you some advice," the officer said to all the soldiers taking the second practice run. "Save your rounds for the closer targets. You only have a certain number of rounds. Why waste them? Even if you miss all the back targets, you'll still pass if you get the close targets."

Before going into the foxhole, Medrano looked intensely at her M-16 and silently spoke to it. "We have not been the greatest friends, but we can change that. I need you to pull through for me, so I can qualify and get out of basic. From this day on, I'm baptizing you Midnight—dark, mysterious, and beautiful."

As targets began popping up, she did not allow herself to become confused or depressed when she missed one. Medrano also took the officer's advice and shot at the nearer targets. She found that by ignoring the far ones, she could hit the closer ones. They seemed to pop up every time a distant target appeared. She had the same number of rounds she needed for all the targets, and she found she needed only one for each because she wasn't shooting the far targets. She was able to hit the closer ones as they popped up .

Medrano finished with some rounds left over. As the officer read out the previous and the new record, he looked extremely surprised when he read Medrano's. She had improved by double, and no one else had shown such a marked improvement. Medrano wanted to tell him she had taken his advice and not to underestimate it. It deflated the good feeling that she had missed qualification by two, and she could not practice anymore. The next time she fired would be to qualify.

That night she fell asleep assuring herself she was going to make it. The next morning she was thrilled she had a full night's sleep without any nightmares.

As third platoon got closer to the qualification range, Medrano tried to beat back her feelings of doubt. She looked at Midnight before getting in the foxhole. In her mind she asked Midnight to do it for her. Thoughts collided in her mind. What makes you think you can do this? What makes you think you can qualify? Shut up!

Medrano quieted her thoughts and started firing. Every time those thoughts came back, she pushed them out. As the targets popped up, she fired and was hitting many of them. If she did not hit one, she refused to allow the bad thoughts to dominate.

The captain read out her name. She qualified! She opened her eyes and drew in a sharp breath. She needed two more to get to sharpshooter since she qualified for the lowest, marksman. The highest was expert. She thought about how much she improved from one day to the next. If only she had even one more day to practice. If only....

"Some of you are disappointed because you didn't get sharpshooter or expert," said Sergeant Washington. "Stop that bullshit! You're going to get the same diploma as a sharpshooter or an expert when you graduate from basic. Be proud of yourselves!" He and Sergeant Acosta started hooking their pinky fingers with the pinkies of the qualifying soldiers and said, "Congratulations!"

Medrano smiled. The "ifs" evaporated in the air. She thought about high school. Back then she would get upset whenever she made anything lower than an "A." She believed her life was worthless and meaningless if she received a "B." Maybe, she thought, you've got to try your best and let it go instead of raking yourself over the coals with "ifs."

"How did you do?" Medrano asked Morningstar who walked by her. Morningstar gave her a big smile and a thumbs up. "I barely qualified a marksman, but I qualified!"

"Great!" exclaimed Medrano.

At the barracks Medrano found there were three who had not qualified. Willet was one of them. Tomorrow they would try to qualify again. If they didn't, they would be recycled.

The following day Sergeant Acosta told them they would be going on bivouac that week.

"What's bivouac?" asked Medrano.

"It's like camping except without the fun," answered Canela.

That night Medrano tried to put bivouac out of her mind. She had never camped in her life. As she tried imagining what camp was like, she saw Willet crying. Medrano went up to Canela.

"What's wrong with her?" whispered Medrano.

"She didn't pass."

"She's going to be recycled?"

"She'll go to another platoon that's in third week."

"At least she doesn't have to start from first week."

"Yes, but she still has to do the gas chamber all over again."

Medrano and Canela stared at each other.

"No wonder she's crying," Medrano said.

"Rumor has it that someone changed her sights."

"You mean messed up her M-16 sights?"

"Yes. I don't know if it's true or not."

"You think someone hated her that much to do something like that?"

"She's stepped on a lot of toes, Medrano."

They looked at Willet whose face was red and puffy. She was not making a sound, but huge tears slid down her face. Willet was sitting alone on her bunk and staring at the wall. The other soldier who had not passed was surrounded by a number of females. They were giving her pep talks.

Sergeant Acosta came out of his office and told third platoon to come to the front. He told them they had to pick buddies for bivouac.

Medrano was looking for Canela when Peck came up to her.

"Would you be my buddy?" Peck asked, not looking directly at Medrano but looking at Willet. Medrano saw everyone pairing up. If she said no, who would pair up with Peck, she wondered.

"I...."

"Please, Med."

"Okay," Medrano found herself saying. She hoped she wouldn't regret it later. "But no sentences that begin with, 'What's wrong with you, Med, is....'"

"I promise."

"I'm serious, Peck," Medrano said sternly.

"My promise is serious too, Med."

At first the web gear with the canteen attached to it, the backpack, the provisions and clothing, the rolled sleeping bag, and the M-16 felt too heavy to carry. Medrano thought she'd never make it, but after a while she began to ignore the load and concentrate on her marching. Soon Medrano would be at her "camp site" for some luxurious days, exactly three days, at the Holiday Basic Training Inn. For the delicate palate, this grand establishment would be serving be C-rations. The presentation was pleasing to the eye. It was not served simply on boring china but in shiny silver cans.

Medrano was longing for one of her mama's tamales when she saw a soldier running by her platoon. She was wearing her gas mask and held a can in the air. Before Medrano fully realized what was happening, her nose started to burn. CS gas! The panic started. She saw Morningstar throwing on her gas mask. She scrambled for her own mask and told herself to calm down. Her face was burning. Her fingers trembled as she pulled the gas mask over her head.

"Damn, double damn!" exclaimed Peck behind her.

With the mask safely on, Medrano turned around. Peck was struggling with her gas mask. Her fingers and body were shaking violently. As Medrano was about to tell her to calm down, Peck ripped off all her gear. Then she ran. Medrano realized that when Peck had yanked off her helmet, her eyeglasses had gone with it. Peck was running somewhere in the woods and was in danger of hitting a tree or something else because she couldn't see.

Medrano looked around to find everything in chaos. Some soldiers had put on their masks. Others were running around frantically. The sergeants looked stunned. They were coughing and gagging. They did not have gas masks. Medrano grabbed Peck's M-16 and ran after her.

"Stop, Peck!"

Peck kept running.

"Stop, before you get us in more trouble!"

Peck stopped suddenly, and Medrano almost ran into her. Medrano was almost hyperventilating. She took off her gas mask. There was no CS gas here. The can had only permeated the area where they had been marching. "

"Med," Peck said squinting, "is that you?"

"Here's your weapon," she said handing it to Peck. "Let's get back pronto!"

"But the gas...."

"There shouldn't be any by now, Peck. We need to get back. The sergeants are distracted. Hopefully they didn't notice you ran off without your M-16!"

"But...."

"Remember what the sergeant said about paying the fiddler if we left our M-16 anywhere?"

Peck's voice shook. "You don't think he'll take it apart and give it to each sergeant, do you?"

"Let's just get back."

"Med."

"What?" Medrano asked, walking away.

"I can't see a thing."

"Hold on to my camouflage jacket."

Medrano walked briskly as Peck followed behind her. When they got back, everything was still in chaos. Medrano grabbed Peck's glasses from the ground and handed them to her. Peck picked up the rest of her gear and put it back on herself.

"You just lucked out, Peck," said Canela.

"Why is that?" asked Peck as her defensive posture began creeping back.

"The sergeants weren't expecting this raid, and the soldier with the can practically ran right under their noses. They're still recovering."

"So?" asked Peck.

"So?! So they didn't see you drop your gear, or your M-16."

"Big deal."

Canela shook her head and laughed. "It's easy to be brave after the storm is over."

"What's that supposed to...."

Sergeant Acosta called to them to get back in formation. Peck eyed Canela angrily before stepping back into position.

When they arrived at the "camp" site, the sergeants told each pair where they were to put up their green tents after chow. This was a beautiful area, Medrano thought as she waited in line for her food. Under normal circumstances it would be fun to be camping here.

Most of the females complained as they opened their cans of C-rations. Medrano did not say anything. She was enjoying the piece of pound cake. And the meat, whatever it was, was not bad.

"Gross, they might as well starve us," said Dekan.

Medrano smiled. Dekan took a mouthful.

"What the hell should be under your fucking chin, huh?" Sergeant Grimes' voice was loud. He was talking to one of his soldiers who was near Medrano. The poor soldier just stared at him stupefied. Medrano looked at her with horror. She had forgotten to snap the strap of her helmet under her chin before she'd stood up. It was okay to unstrap it to eat, but it better be strapped when a soldier stood.

"You're an idiot!" Sergeant Grimes yelled. "A sorry-assed idiot! You're even stupider than you look! From day one you haven't done a damn thing right, Johnson! You're a loser! A complete loser with a capital L! LOSER!"

Medrano thought, smoke her, but don't strip her of every shred of dignity she has. She looked for the other sergeants.

"You'll never be able to tell your ass from your brain!"

Johnson's face was turning blue, as if she had stopped breathing. Her body was trembling.

"How the hell am I supposed to teach a stupid, empty-headed bitch like you anything? Where the hell were you when God was giving out brains? Fucking somebody?"

The skin around Jackson's eyes started twitching in rapid movements, and her chest heaved up and down as if unable to stop. Medrano's insides burned even more than they had in the gas chamber.

"I'll fucking have to cram some brains into you myself! Be in my tent after chow tonight, and we'll see if I don't smoke your sorry ass until you lose your stupidity!"

"Why does she have to go to your tent, Sergeant Grimes?" asked

Canela angrily.

"Who the hell gave you permission to fucking speak, Canela? You are even stupider than this one!"

"I...."

"I've had about all I can take from you idiot soldiers." By the time I get through with you, you'll fucking be begging for mercy!"

"May I speak to you, Sergeant Grimes?" asked Sergeant Duke, a female drill sergeant from another platoon. She had walked into the area unnoticed and had been observing the scene.

Sergeant Grimes looked at Sergeant Duke angrily.

"I'm not through with you yet, Canela! Johnson!"

The sergeants walked a few yards away. Although Medrano couldn't hear what they were saying, she was sure they were talking about the episode with Johnson. They kept pointing at her.

Canela put her hands on her hips and glared at Sergeant Grimes. Medrano then noticed Peck had a strange look on her face. Her lower lip was trembling.

A couple of sergeants and the captain walked into the area and stared at Johnson. She was still shaking, and several soldiers from her platoon had surrounded her.

"What's going on?" Sergeant Acosta asked.

Sergeant Grimes yelled, "Bitch! Cunt!" and then slapped Sergeant Duke so hard she fell. After a couple of seconds, she stood up and looked as if she was going to kill him. By that time, Sergeant Acosta and the captain ran in between them.

The sergeants quickly moved the soldiers in formation, and they marched away. Sergeant Washington took third platoon to their area and ordered them to put up their tents. As Peck and Medrano were buttoning the two halves of the tent together, Medrano thought Peck was being uncharacteristically quiet.

"Grimes is such a sleaze," Medrano said. Peck only nodded slightly. "I wonder what's going to happen to him?"

Peck's face was stone. "I don't know, and I don't care."

"I can't believe he...."

"Let's finish putting up the tent, okay?"

"I...."

"I'm not in the mood to talk right now," Peck cut in. Medrano had never seen Peck's eyes look so sad.

Peck kept working, and Medrano started doing the same thing. They finished, and the only meager words exchanged had been about putting the tent together.

Sergeant Washington inspected the tent. "Dig the trench right here," Sergeant Washington said, digging his boot into the earth.

"Trench?" asked Medrano after the sergeant had left.

"In the event it rains," Peck answered. She grabbed one of the small trowels and started to dig.

They were almost finished when Sergeant Acosta walked up to them.

"You're digging it too close to the tent."

Medrano spoke right away. "Sergeant Washington told...."

"Cover the trench up and start again," he yelled as he walked away.

Medrano looked at Peck and rolled her eyes. "Back to the old drawing board."

They covered the trench, and started re-digging it farther from the tent. Sergeant Washington walked over to them.

"Is this where I told you to dig the trench."

"No, sergeant, but...."

"But my ass!"

"Sergeant Acosta told us to dig it...."

"I don't care what Sergeant Acosta told you! I care about what I told you! Cover the trench and dig it closer to the tent," he yelled, stomping away.

"I can't believe this," Medrano said.

Peck didn't say a word. She started covering up the trench and digging the other one.

"What are you doing?" Sergeant Acosta yelled.

Peck just looked at him.

"Sergeant Washington said...."

"Do I look like I give a shit about what Sergeant Washington said. Dig the damn trench where I told you to dig it." He walked away in a huff.

"This is not really happening. We're in some play somewhere performing a comedy of errors!" Medrano exclaimed.

Peck started covering the trench again. Medrano started digging another one.

"What the hell is this. You two need to do what I tell you to do," Sergeant Washington shouted.

"Yes, sergeant," said Medrano.

"Dig this right here," he screamed, digging his boot in the earth again. "And I want no more bullshit from you." He strode away.

Medrano put down her shovel and sat. She folded her arms across her chest and stared at the earth. Peck covered up the trench.

"Third platoon. Formation."

"Saved by the bell," Medrano said sarcastically.

They assembled in formation and marched to a room filled with all kinds of weapons. Sergeant Washington told them that they would have to clean and grease the weapons. It was their platoon's turn.

"Great," whispered Canela. "While the other platoons get to sleep, we get to do this."

They started on the weapons and felt wearier with every passing minute. Fortunately the sergeants were outside, so the soldiers could talk with ease.

"What do you think will happen to Grimes?" Medrano asked Canela as they were cleaning weapons in what seemed to be a big pan of oil.

"I don't know, but I hope he really gets his."

"I'm glad the captain was there to see him hit the sergeant," Medrano said.

"I hope it's true that whatever goes around, comes around."

"I firmly believe that, Adela."

Canela looked at Peck who was quietly greasing some weapons on the other side of the room.

"What's up with her?" Canela asked.

"I have no idea. She's hardly said a word to me."

"She's got some deep-seated problems."

"I've stopped trying to figure Peck out," Medrano stated.

They finally finished at midnight, and Medrano never imagined she would be so happy to see a tent. Peck didn't say a word as they got in their sleeping bags. They were still in their fatigues.

"Goodnight," Medrano said.

"Goodnight," Peck said as she turned her back to Medrano.

Medrano closed her eyes. She snuggled deep into her sleeping bag but still felt cold. She couldn't help her teeth from chattering. Her papa had always told her she got cold easily, and she always thought he exaggerated. Now she thought he may have been right.

Medrano kept going in and out of a rocky sleep. She finally sat up in anger, turned on her flashlight, and pulled on another pair of socks to see if that would help. Peck rolled over, facing Medrano, and appeared to be fast asleep. Medrano thought about how different Peck looked in her sleep. With her glasses off, her face seemed soft somehow. Almost innocent and fragile.

Rain started falling. Great, Medrano thought, we never did finish digging the stupid trench. But the rain was more of a light sprinkle, so she lay down again and listened to the gentle thumping on the tent. It reminded her of when she hugged her mama and could hear her heart. In a few minutes, she fell into a nice, peaceful sleep.

"Stop hitting her!" screamed Peck.

Medrano woke up abruptly. For a couple of seconds, she tried to figure out what was happening. She wasn't sure where she was.

"Stop it." Peck's voice shot through the dark. "No. Give me the gun!"

"Peck, wake up!" Medrano exclaimed as she sat up and turned on her flashlight.

"Please give it to me, Dad."

"Wake up."

What else can I do wondered Medrano. If she shook her, Peck might hit her as she did the last time.

There was a shrill pain in Peck's voice that reminded Medrano of a hurt animal, "Mom!" she sobbed.

"Wake up, Peck."

Peck started whispering desperately, "Don't die. Please don't die."

"Peck!"

"How could you kill her? "Peck started shaking violently. "Mom!"

"Peck!"

Suddenly, Peck's eyes opened. She looked around as if she was trying to place where she was. Her eyes landed on Medrano who was looking at her with horror, her mouth forming an "o."

"What are you staring at?" asked Peck, wiping perspiration from herself.

"I'm sorry, Peck."

"About what?"

"Your mother."

Peck glared at Medrano. "What about my mother?"

"You know," said Medrano uncomfortably.

"What?"

"Your father...The gun...."

Peck was shocked. "How did you...," she stammered.

"You talked in your sleep, Peck. You talked during your nightmare."

Anger twisted Peck's face. "Why don't you stop eavesdropping on people's dreams, Medrano."

Medrano rolled her eyes. "It's not like I could help it. We're sleeping in the same tent."

"Forget what you heard, Med. Let's get some sleep," she said.

"For all it's worth, Peck. I'm sorry about your mamacita."

"Don't be," Peck mumbled angrily.

"What?"

Peck swiftly turned over to face Medrano. "It was her own fault my father shot her."

"Why...."

Peck sat up. "She stayed in the fucking marriage."

Medrano also sat up. "Why?"

"She should've left him. How many times did I see him hit her? How many times did I see him slap her around? He treated her like a side of beef. He yelled at her and abused her mentally and physically. Why did she stay?"

"Maybe...."

"She was weak. That's what it was," stated Peck.

"Maybe she didn't have enough self-confidence to leave."

"She was a fucking weakling!" Peck exclaimed.

"Maybe your father robbed her of every sense of self she had. Maybe every time she thought of leaving, she thought she couldn't make it in the world. Maybe your father had ingrained that idea in her. Maybe he threatened to kill her if she left. Maybe she felt she didn't have a choice. Maybe he threatened to kill you her child, Peck."

"How the hell would you know?"

"I've done research papers on battered women. I've visited shelters."

"Does that make you a fucking expert?"

"I also have a cousin whose husband used to hit her, and her face would always be black and blue," said Medrano.

"Used to? Did she leave him?"

"Eventually. After a long while, she got the guts to leave him; but then he stalked her."

"And?"

"One day he took a gun and shot her and then shot himself. Luckily, she lived, and he died."

"Well my mom wasn't so lucky."

"What happened to your dad?"

"Life in jail. I put him there," Peck said sadly.

"You did?"

"He tried to say it didn't happen like it happened, but I was the only witness."

"You did the right thing," said Medrano.

"He was a jerk, and my mom...."

"Don't blame your mom, Peck."

"I really don't want to talk about this anymore. Forget this conversation, and let's get some sleep," Peck turned again.

Medrano could not go back to sleep. She was almost certain Peck was not asleep either. It was time to get up, even though it was still dark outside. She could feel the bags under her eyes and the yawns stuck in her throat.

Medrano sat up. She probably should change her underwear, but she was so cold she could not bring herself to do it. She couldn't even comb her hair. Good thing it was still in a bun. She did force herself to put on her deodorant. She stuck her hand up her shirt and smoothed it on. The rose scent filled her nose and for a moment made her feel a little better.

With flashlights in hand, Medrano and Peck started tearing down the tent. Sergeant Acosta had said they would sleep the first night of bivouac in a tent, and the second night they would sleep without one. Medrano did not want to think about sleeping out in the cold.

"About last night, Med."

174

"Yes?"

"Don't you mention it to anybody. Forget it."

"Okay, if that's how you want it." An orange-yellow sun started rising. Medrano couldn't help thinking how pretty the new day was, in spite of all the sadness already born into it.

After chow and PT, third platoon was marched to a range where they practiced moving their buddies. They pretended as if they were in a war and practiced moving each other in the frontlines. While Medrano was behind a tree, she pointed at Peck who was directly opposite from her under a bush. Then Medrano pointed ahead. This signaled Peck to move forward while Medrano covered her with her M-16. Then Peck would do the same for Medrano until they reached a specified site.

The sergeant in charge of the range told Medrano she had done a good job, but he told Peck she needed to get her head out of her ass. Peck had lost her concentration several times and had forgotten to keep her eye on Medrano. Medrano was then forced to shout, "Buddy, are you ready?"

During chow Medrano sat with Canela, García, and Dekan. Instead of C-rations they were given a paper bag with a ham sandwich and a brownie.

"I kind of miss the C-rations," said Medrano.

"You've got strange taste buds," said Canela.

"Real strange," said Dekan.

Medrano chuckled. "I suppose you're right."

Canela's eyes turned dreamy. "The only thing I miss are enchiladas. I dreamed about them last night."

Medrano looked at Peck who was eating by herself. Peck seemed to want to be rid of Medrano. She had made it obvious she did not want to stand next to Medrano in the chow line.

They finished eating and heard in the distance, first platoon being called for formation. After a while they heard second platoon.

"Our turn next," said Canela.

They waited but didn't hear a call for their platoon.

"Third Platoon!"

"Finally," said Dekan.

They jumped up and ran toward the formation area where some of the soldiers where already in position. As soon as they reached their positions, Sergeant Acosta said, "Those who were already here, standfast. The rest of you, down!"

Medrano was stunned. She went down in pushup position, putting her M-16 over her hands.

"Up, up, up!"

What was going on, she thought? Why was he smoking them?

"Down!"

Medrano's equipment felt as if it weighed a ton while she jumped up and down in squat thrusts.

"That'll fucking teach you not to listen when I'm ordering you to formation. What took you so long to get here?"

"But...," One of the females started to say.

"I don't want to hear any explanations. Up, up, up!"

They had not heard him. Was it their fault his voice had not carried? Most of the soldiers had not heard him calling to them. There were only a few standing fast and not being punished.

"Down, down, down!"

This went on for about ten minutes, and Medrano's face was dripping with sweat. Her equipment felt heavier and heavier. Finally, Sergeant Acosta told them to do the pushups. They were easier than thrusts but still required almost superhuman strength with the web gear, the back pack, and the weapon loaded on a soldier's back.

He finally let them stand. A deep sigh quietly stirred among them. Medrano could not stop shaking when she stood up.

"Now it's my turn," Sergeant Washington yelled, and he proceeded to smoke them for another fifteen minutes as Sergeant Acosta had.

Medrano's stomach was burning. Her eyes saw red specks, and her nostrils flared. Some of the "hard core" females, the toughest ones, were silently crying. A sense of helplessness and unfairness was sitting in the air. Medrano let her anger evaporate any tears. Not one teardrop fell from her eyes. The the only moisture on her face was from the rain.

They finally started marching. Sergeant Acosta loudly sang cadence, but the soldiers sang in low voices. For once the sergeants did not push it.

At the end of the day, the sergeants told them to pick a foxhole and sleep in it. A number of shallow foxholes dotted the area. They were not half as deep as the ones from which Medrano had shot her M-16. She dreaded spending the night there; trying to get some z's would be nearly impossible. In this cold, would she wake up in the morning; or would she have to be thawed out? Visions of frostbite raced through her mind.

Canela, García, Dekan, Morningstar, and two other females were in one huge foxhole.

"Room for one more?" asked Medrano.

"Get your ass in here," said Dekan.

Medrano scurried into the foxhole where they opened their sleeping bags and spread them across each other. It was very toasty, and Medrano couldn't feel the cold at all. Nearby, Peck had slipped into a foxhole by herself.

"Peck, why don't you sleep with us?" called Medrano.

"I don't think so."

"You're going to freeze over there by yourself."

"I'll be fine," Peck said sternly.

"Suit yourself." Medrano decided that she couldn't do anything for a person who did not want to be helped.

The night was beautiful. There was a full moon, the sky was clear, and Medrano could see a zillion stars.

"My bod still smarts from that whipping we took today," Dekan said.

"No kidding!" Canela exclaimed. "I thought I was going to die."

García put her hands over her face. "Die? I thought I was already dead."

"I don't know what was worse getting smoked like we were today or the gas chamber," remarked Morningstar.

"That reminds me," said Dekan, taking out her gas mask. "I'm wearing my gas mask in case the sergeants throw us some gas cans. Remember yesterday?"

"Do you think they would do such a cruel thing?" asked García.

"They did say we'd be getting some surprise raids during bivouac—to test us if we're prepared for them," Morningstar reflected.

"I don't know about you guys, but I'm not taking any risks. I'm going to be able to put this thing on fast. I don't want to get even a whiff of that shit." Dekan put on her mask.

"Me either," said Canela.

All of them started putting on their gas masks. When the other soldiers in the other foxholes saw what they were doing, they followed suit.

Medrano ignored the uncomfortable mask and stared at the sky. Then she realized she had to go to the bathroom.

"The nearest latrine is far, isn't it?" asked Medrano. She dreaded going to an outside latrine where she would have to sit on a smelly, bottomless pit.

"You have to go?" asked Canela. "

"Yes."

"If I were you, I'd go behind a tree," said Dekan.

Medrano didn't like that idea. "But the sergeant might be inspecting or something and...."

"And see you with your pants down!" Dekan exclaimed. She giggled loudly, "See your cheeks."

"I'll just hold it in."

"Just because you're scared of a man seeing your ass?"

"So what if I don't like strangers seeing my rear," Medrano said defensively.

"It's only some fat and a slice in between, but I guess you being a virgin makes you...."

Medrano pointed her index finger at her. "I'm not apologizing for being a virgin, okay?"

"Calm down, Medrano. I didn't mean to piss you off. I think it's neat that you've never screwed anyone, that you're waiting for the right moment."

"That's what, deep inside, I know is the right thing to do," Medrano said.

Dekan nodded. "I was fifteen when I made love for the first time, and I've never done it with anyone else."

"Sammy?" Medrano's face grew red as she thought about the letter she read over Dekan's shoulder.

"Yes, Sammy," she said sighing. Dekan fell asleep soon after. Medrano imagined she was dreaming of Sammy since she kept saying, "luv you," in her sleep.

While it was better than the Peck episode, she wished she didn't have to eavesdrop on other people's dreams. It made her feel like an intruder, but she was having a hard time going to sleep.

Finally Medrano's eyelids grew heavy. She drifted off. Soon her dreams began. She was in the desert watching a spectacular sunrise. The gray of the sand sparkled, and the yuccas pointed at her. Her family was in the distance smiling at her. Suddenly the skies grew dark, and thunder crashed. She woke up before the water came crashing down.

Medrano's bladder was about to burst. She checked her watch. It was 1:00 a.m. She had just spent a couple of hours needing to relieve herself and with a stupid gas mask. Enough was enough. She jumped up, yanked off her mask, grabbed her flashlight, and doubletimed it to a bush some distance from the nearest foxhole. Unbuttoning her fatigues, she started to release her bladder. To her relief she made it to a squat position. She didn't stop urinating for a long time.

For one thing she was grateful, Medrano thought; she wasn't on her period. She wouldn't want to leave a pool of urine mixed with blood. The urine was bad enough. Also, having to change pads during bivouac would've been a nightmare. The latrines they were using were outside, albeit new models unlike the old-fashioned ones her grandmother once had in Mexico. Nevertheless, they were still smelly and nasty.

Before basic Medrano had worried about how she would handle her menstrual period in the military. But like some of her other worries, her monthly cycle had taken a backseat to other pressing activities. The many pockets in her uniform had made it easy to store pads. Most of the other females were using tampons, which seemed easier. Medrano had tried them once and found them too painful to use.

Because of how strenuous basic training was, some of the soldiers weren't having periods at all. Medrano couldn't count on such luck since her cycle never missed a month. One thing she could consider herself fortunate about was that she rarely had cramps. Considering what Sergeant Acosta had said about the matter, she was lucky indeed.

"Anyone bitching and moaning about cramps will get PT right then and there. I know for a fact exercise is good for that sort of thing, so don't even try to fool me!"

"Nice to fucking know that Sergeant Acosta's cock turns into a vagina once a month, and he knows how we feel," whispered Peck.

Medrano smiled and subconsciously nodded her head as she thought of Peck's comment. It brought her back to the matter at hand. Thinking of Sergeant Acosta made her urinate faster in case he appeared. She finally finished. When Medrano refastened her fatigues, she felt life was good.

She walked back to the foxhole. As she snuggled in, she noticed Peck was at the end, next to Dekan sleeping like a baby. It struck Medrano how funny they looked all in one hole. Heads were coming out of all sides of the foxhole since no one was sleeping in the same position. Medrano had her feet on both sides.

"Anyone take off their gas mask?" asked Dekan who was lying opposite of Medrano.

"I did."

"Who is that?"

"Medrano."

"Are you sure there's no CS gas out there?"

"Positive," Medrano said.

"But I heard a swishing sound out there, Medrano."

"It was me urinating."

"Damn, Medrano, you sounded like a damn waterfall," Dekan stated.

"What do you expect? I held it in for hours."

"So you took off your gas mask?"

"For the 20 millionth time, yes. There's no gas out there."

"Let me see," she said, sitting up and touching Medrano's face.

"You don't trust me?"

"It's not personal, Medrano. It's just that I wouldn't even trust Mother Teresa when it comes to CS gas."

Dekan took off her mask. Soon both she and Medrano fell into a deep sleep.

"Rise and shine!" Canela exclaimed.

Waking up, Medrano felt a numbing pain in her right shoulder. It felt like her foot had when she was put on profile. It looked normal, but it did not feel good.

During breakfast chow in the field, the females were talkative all except Medrano.

"You're more quiet than usual, Medrano," said Dekan.

"I'm wondering whether to go on sick call or not."

"Are you sick, Medrano?" asked Canela.

"My shoulder is really bothering me."

Dekan swung her head up and down. "I bet it was that fucking whipping we took yesterday. I don't know why the hell they dogged us with all our equipment on. No wonder you're sick."

"Talking about sick people, did anybody see Grimes at all yesterday?" asked García.

Everyone said no.

"I didn't even see him this morning," said Morningstar.

García looked as if she was in deep thought. "I've seen Sergeant Duke but not him."

"Yes. I hadn't thought about it, but she's been around," said Dekan.

"Do you think he's gone for good?" asked Morningstar.

"Let's hope so!" Canela exclaimed, "But...."

"But what?" asked García. "

I don't think he's gone for good," Canela stated angrily.

"You don't think so?" asked García. "But we haven't seen him.

"I think they shipped him someplace else."

"You really think so?" asked Dekan.

"He'll be sexually harassing some other soldiers," hissed Canela.

Silence took the moment. They stared at each other sadly.

When the sergeants began calling sick call, Medrano decided to go. As she was herded onto the cattle truck, she noticed Dekan on it too. A sergeant stared at the soldiers, daring them to speak. Medrano clamped her jaws tight, and wondered why Dekan was on sick call. I bet she's not really sick at all, thought Medrano. She's riding sick call so she can get out of the last day of bivouac.

After they got their files, they went to the clinic and waited. Dekan sat next to her. Medrano stared straight ahead at the wall. She was messaging her shoulder when she heard snoring. She turned to find Dekan fast asleep, sitting straight up in the chair. Her snoring had a deep nasal quality. The other soldiers were silently snickering. Medrano was relieved no one in authority was around. She quickly poked Dekan. Her eyes flew open.

"You'll get in trouble if they catch you sleeping," quickly whispered Medrano.

Dekan nodded to her. Her eyes looked blank, and her face looked as if she was in another world. A nurse walked in and called the next person. She went in and all the soldiers rose and moved up a chair. Dekan would be next to see the doctor. Medrano stared at the front wall again. She also thought about how tired she was. Bivouac was an exhausting experience even though she had slept half decently last night. Then she heard it again! Snoring! Medrano turned to look at Dekan in astonishment. The other females were having difficulty stifling their laughs.

"Wake up," Medrano whispered as she poked her again.

Dekan woke up in the middle of a gnarly snore. Medrano shook her head at her, and Dekan kept blinking her eyes rapidly. After a few seconds, her blinking slowed down. This time Medrano saw it coming. At Dekan's first snore, Medrano poked her again. Dekan opened her eyes wide and did not blink for a few seconds. She fought sleep, quickly opening her eyes whenever they slid shut. But soon closed and the snoring quickly followed.

Medrano poked her again. "Psst."

Dekan opened her eyes just as the nurse came in and called her to see the doctor. How lucky can you get, thought Medrano. If it had been me, I probably would have been caught on the first snore.

It was nice to sit quietly without having to poke someone every couple of seconds. Medrano knew she should be studying her smart book but could not bring herself to do it. Her mind drifted to her mama. She had talked to her just before leaving on bivouac. Her mama had told her she had been praying for her, but Medrano did not need to be told. She could feel those prayers. Medrano could even see them, especially when it rained.

Thank you God for helping me survive bivouac.

Thank you God for helping me qualify with the grenade and M-16.

Thank you for leading me out of that gas chamber.

Thank you....

Dekan came out of the office carrying two armfuls of medicine. Medrano felt guilty for thinking she was "riding" sick call. That was probably why she had been having trouble keeping her eyes open. She really was sick, extremely sick.

When Medrano saw the doctor, she explained that her drill sergeants had dogged them; and now her shoulder felt horrible. He said it was probably nothing but a strained shoulder and gave her some Ben-Gay. As Medrano walked out, she could not believe that was all he had given her.

Medrano thought she would be taken back to bivouac. Instead she and the rest of the sick-call soldiers in her battalion were taken to KP. She wished they had been allowed to go back to the barracks to shower and change. It had been a couple of days since she had changed her underwear. She had never gone a day without changing her undergarments in her entire life. She tried not to stand close to anyone for fear they could smell her.

Medrano spent the day doing what she usually did in KP—cleaning. At one point she went into the latrine and found Dekan asleep. She was snoring happily on the floor in one of the stalls. When KP duty was over, Medrano again thought about Dekan's luck. No one had caught her.

When she and Dekan returned to the barracks, they found everything in total chaos. The mirrors had shaving cream, bunks were torn apart, and the trash cans were upside down, trash thrown everywhere.

"I can't believe this!" Medrano exclaimed. "The sergeants are jerks."

"I know we haven't been keeping up with the barracks, but what did they expect? We came back from the ranges late. Where did they think we'd find the time to keep it clean?"

"They expect us to get absolutely no sleep."

First they showered and then helped reassemble one another's bunks. After cleaning their area, they sat down and talked.

"I've got to apologize to you, Dekan. I thought you were riding sick call. When you came out with all that medication, I knew I was wrong."

Dekan laughed. "That's the funny part. I'm not sick at all, but they gave me a ton of medicine. I was just trying to get out of the last day of bivouac."

"I'm really sick, and all they gave me was this," Medrano said, showing her the Ben-Gay. Dekan couldn't stop laughing.

Peacetime: Spirit of the Eagle

The soldiers came back from bivouac. Dekan and Medrano had straightened out some of the mess by then.

Medrano helped Canela as she reassembled her bunk.

"You know how we slept with those stupid, uncomfortable gas masks last night?" asked Canela.

"Yes."

"We were terrified that the sergeants would spray us with the gas."

"Yes," said Medrano.

"They decided not to surprise spray us. They felt bad about making us stay up the night before, cleaning the weapons."

"We slept with the stupid things for nothing?"

"Yep," Canela said.

They could not stop laughing.

"Oh, well," Medrano said, flinging her hands in the air. We're at the end of the week. Two more weeks and we'll be through!"

Sixth Week

I t was nerve racking not knowing where they were going or what they would be doing. The sergeants smiled knowingly at each other as they stood in formation but didn't tell the soldiers what to expect. A sudden, awful thought rushed through Medrano's mind. They were going back to the gas chamber. She immediately pushed it aside. Then she saw the other females' faces and knew they had the same fear. The sergeants had laughed openly at their somber faces.

Medrano tried to relax and empty her mind as they marched. She couldn't do it. She kept wondering if this was the way to the chamber. This trail looked the same as all the other ones. More than ever before, Medrano regretted having no sense of direction.

As they marched out of the dirt trails and onto a paved road, Medrano felt her whole body relax. She sensed the relief in all of them. The sergeant stopped in front of a movie theater. Medrano wondered what class they would be taking. The last time they had been there, they had learned how to identify different types of terrain.

"Sergeant Washington and I decided since you were doing well, we'd let you watch a movie."

Medrano had to bite her lower lip. Her mouth had almost dropped wide open.

"There is one condition to this," said Sergeant Washington. "All of you will have to watch the same film. Get in line, third platoon. Buy your tickets."

Medrano got in line. Morningstar kept fidgeting behind her.

"What's wrong?" asked Medrano.

Morningstar was debating whether to tell her and kept looking at the line which was getting shorter. She finally whispered, "I don't have any money, Medrano."

"I'll cover you, Morningstar."

"I can't...."

"Tell you what. When we graduate next week, I'd like my footwear super shiny. I can't ever get them gleaming like you get yours. I'll pay your way if you shine my dress shoes."

Sergeant Acosta had told them they would be getting dress uniforms soon with dress footwear. Whoever passed would graduate in them.

Morningstar smiled. "That's a deal."

Inside, Medrano bought a large popcorn and sodas for herself and for Morningstar. When they sat down, Medrano realized she had been so excited she never thought about what they were going to watch.

"What's the movie, Morningstar?" Morningstar chuckled. "I have no idea."

The theater darkened, and the American flag appeared on the screen. "The Star Spangled Banner" played. Everyone shot up and stood at attention. When the music ended, everyone sat down and watched previews for future movies. Then the flag appeared on the screen again. Some soldiers quickly stood at attention. Medrano was debating whether she should stand up when the sergeant screamed.

"Sit down you knuckleheads. That's the beginning of the movie."

The soldiers plopped themselves down, and laughter was heard. The movie was about a haunted house. In civilian life Medrano would never be caught dead watching a movie like that. It was too scary. Once she had been out with her most beloved boyfriend who had insisted they see a slasher movie. He said they always went to see movies she wanted, so she relented. That night she was not able to sleep.

The next time he suggested a horror movie, she said, "No way." He kept insisting they see it. She finally asked him why he wanted her to see it so badly since he could go with friends. It was because he wanted Medrano to consider him her knight in shining armor—her protector. Medrano realized something that night. He always wanted to tell her what to do and what to think. She broke up with him, telling him he needed to be a baby-sitter instead of a boyfriend.

That was the last time Medrano saw a horror film. When this movie ended, Medrano was not scared at all. Now there were experiences that were scarier than any movie, experiences, such as the gas chamber and passing basic. That night in her bunk, Medrano didn't relive the scary parts of the film as she had in the past.

"I almost died when they took us to the theater," said Canela.

"I thought we were going someplace awful!" Dekan exclaimed.

"Talking about awful, have any of you seen Grimes?"

"No."

"At least we're safe from him for the time being."

"Medrano, can I speak to you privately?" asked Peck.

"Sure."

Medrano did not like her aggressive tone. She followed Peck through the double doors to the balcony overlooking the formation area.

"You've been looking at me strangely," said Peck with narrow eyes.

"I'm just concerned that you're okay."

"Why the hell wouldn't I be okay?"

"You've been through a horrendous ordeal with your mom."

"So you feel sorry for me."

"No. I feel bad for you."

"What the fuck is the difference?" Peck demanded.

"Can't I be compassionate towards...."

"No. I don't need you to feel 'bad' for me. I told you once to forget that night at bivouac."

"I guess you don't need anybody!" exclaimed Medrano.

"All people are good for is to hurt you."

"Do you really believe that, Peck?"

Peck stared at Medrano angrily. "There's nothing to fucking indicate otherwise as far as I am concerned."

"If you don't need anybody, then why did you join the Army where you'd be surrounded by people all the time? You didn't need the money."

Peck was taken aback. "I....."

"Maybe people are not useless. Maybe it's okay to feel for each other."

Peck's eyes narrowed again as she regained her composure. "This is the last time I tell you. Stop feeling sorry for me. I told you! Forget that night at bivouac!" Peck exclaimed, stomping off. As she was about to open the double doors, she turned around, "Besides, you're the one without any money. I'm the one who is rich. Maybe I should feel sorry for you." Peck swung the doors open and walked in.

The problem with a statement like that, thought Medrano, is that not even Peck believes it.

This time third platoon knew where they were marching. They were going to another obstacle course which was the Victory Tower. When they arrived, Medrano smiled. It was nothing compared to the other obstacle course. For one thing it wasn't nearly as large. In fact, it looked more like a giant park.

They walked across a log supported by two stumps, about waist high above the ground. When Dekan got on, she started shaking her behind. Everyone roared.

"Get your ass across the log, and stop screwing around," said Sergeant Washington.

Morningstar trembled as she moved across. But she did it.

"She's going to pass basic on sheer will," said Canela, looking at Morningstar with admiration.

"Where's the other height lover?" asked Dekan sarcastically.

"Who?"

"Peck."

"She went on sick call," said Canela.

Dekan laughed loudly. "Oh, I'm sure she's real sick."

They climbed, crawled, and swung. Medrano enjoyed it. What she did not enjoy was march practice when they got back to the barracks area. They would be competing for best platoon early the following week. They would also have to do a few nifty tricks with the M-16, moving them in unison while marching.

"I'll tell you something, third platoon, males cannot march better than females," said Sergeant Acosta. "When a group of females walk somewhere together, they march on the same foot without even knowing it. Sergeant Washington and I have been watching you. You're the best marchers we've ever had."

"We've never seen anybody march like you can," he said. "And there's no damn reason we shouldn't win next week."

They continued practicing. The sergeants started calling some of the soldiers out. Only the best would be allowed to compete. Medrano kept waiting for them to take remove her. She saw them take out Morningstar and several of the others. Finally she was taken out, and her whole body relaxed. She went to sit on the ground by Morningstar and the others.

"Why'd you give up?" Morningstar whispered.

"What?"

"I mean, I know I can't march, but you can."

"I can't either," said Medrano.

"Yes, you can. You just don't want the responsibility."

"What?"

"You don't want the responsibility of going against your insecurities. You want to stay where it's safe."

Medrano thought of high school. The only time she ever enjoyed P.E. was when the teacher introduced the class to volleyball. There was something about thumping that ball that she loved. One day her teacher had suggested she join the school volleyball team. Medrano looked at the teacher as if she had just said the craziest thing in the world. "Am I good enough for that?"

"You are a fantastic player, Eliza."

"But I've never been good at anything physical."

"You can really play volleyball."

Medrano found the guts out for the team. But while she was waiting for tryouts, she convinced herself she would fail. She hadn't failed at many things. Her grades were top notch, and she had numerous certificates and awards. She walked out of the gym then.

Medrano looked at Morningstar. "If you never try, then you can't fail."

"Really?"

"I mean that if you don't give it your all and you fail, it's not like you didn't try. You tried your best anyway."

"What's wrong with failing anyway?"

Sergeant Acosta gave them a look, and they shut their mouths.

"I'm so happy this day is finally here!" exclaimed García.

They had just received their class A uniforms and were hanging them in their lockers. Medrano smiled. She knew exactly what García meant. The fact that they had received their dress uniforms wasn't a big deal. It was because their arrival marked the beginning of their sixth week. At zero week, as their fatigues were thrown at them, they had stared forlornly at the soldiers getting their dress uniforms. Now in sixth week their uniforms weren't thrown at them. They had a confident air about them. They chatted with each other, smiled, and chuckled. In zero week the new soldiers wouldn't look at each other, much less smile.

"Did you see how those new recruits looked at us?" asked García, as she laughed.

"Their poor, little eyes were darting towards us," said Canela.

"Poor suckers. They don't know what they're in for."

Medrano caressed the uniform. She would graduate in a white, cotton shirt with a black piece under the front collar; dark green, crisp pants; and shiny, black shoes. She was issued a plain purse, black and square. To top it all off, she received a smart, little black hat with a gold eagle emblem.

"We've almost finished paying the piper We're almost finished!" Medrano exclaimed excitedly.

Walker called a meeting in the dayroom, and everyone hurried there.

"The sergeants decided we're going to the Cadence Club tonight," Walker said. There were yelps of joy. "We'll be leaving in about half an hour."

Medrano walked back to her locker with Canela. "What's with the sergeants this week? First a movie and then the Cadence Club.

Did they take a nice pill or what?"

"They don't have to be as strict now that it's almost over."

Medrano put on fresh fatigues. When she saw other females putting on some make-up, she decided to risk it. She did not have any with her, so she borrowed some from García. In civilian life, she had rarely worn make-up only on special occasions. She figured this qualified as one. She wore only brown eyeshadow and was delighted to find a rich, dark color. It blended well with her natural-bronze skin tone and gave her a warm look. She dabbed on light red lipstick that made her lips look flushed rather than made up.

Outside in formation Sergeant Acosta slowly walked past each one as they stood at attention.

"My, my don't we look different today!" he exclaimed.

Sergeant Washington nodded. "Some rules before we go. Absolutely no drinking. No leaving the club except for standing outside if you want. No dancing with males. No speaking to males. No fraternizing. They are off limits to you, soldiers."

Third platoon arrived at the Cadence Club, a plain club with a wooden dance floor. There wasn't much they could do, so Medrano played video games. The others played pool. She sipped a Coke, relishing the moment. Not much time had been allowed solely for entertainment. But after a while, she became bored and walked outside where there was a group of females talking to the sergeants. They were laughing.

"There was this man and his sister in Mexico who were very poor," said Sergeant Acosta, "One day...."

"But I thought you were Puerto Rican," said a soldier.

"I am," he stated.

"You know Mexican jokes?"

Sergeant Acosta looked at the sky. "Please help me have patience with these knuckleheads." He looked back at the soldier, "I know all kinds of jokes. Anyway, one day the man decided he was going to the U.S. to make his fortune. After many years in the United States, he decided to share his riches with his sister who was still in Mexico. He opened his closet, pointed at himself, and said, 'What clothes this vato has.' Vato loosely means dude. Anyway, as he walked outside, he said, 'What a house this vato, has.' He climbed into his car and said, 'What a car this dude has.' He drove to Mexico where he found his sister was a nun in a convent. When he asked her to come with him, she said, 'I can't. I'm now married to God.' Then the guy said, 'What a brother-in-law this dude has!'"

Everyone laughed hard, especially Medrano. She looked at the sergeants and thought for the first time how handsome they were. The thought had never passed through her mind before.

When they arrived back at the barracks, Medrano snuggled in her bunk. She closed her eyes and did not think of anything negative. Soon a deep, smooth sleep overtook her.

When she woke up in the morning, the first thought that came to her was that they would have the 15-mile march that day. She did not want to be reminded she had problems marching for a couple of miles with full gear, much less for 15 miles.

Deal with it, kept resonating in her mind.

When they were in formation ready to go, she could tell others were dreading it too.

"Since today is going to be a hot day, we're going to allow you to take off your fatigue jackets, and march in your T-shirts," said Sergeant Washington.

When they ran upstairs to leave their jackets they couldn't believe it. Never had they been allowed to march in their T-shirts. They returned to formation and were marched in back of second platoon. The whole battalion was on the 15-mile march that day. A sergeant from another platoon sang cadence, but the sergeant couldn't keep the rhythm. The soldiers ended up on wrong feet and stepping on each other.

"Damn, double damn," whispered Peck.

Medrano thought how impossible this situation would be for 15 miles. When they arrived at a bridge, they were stopped. Then the sergeants got the soldiers in one line, and they started walking. After calmly strolling for 15 minutes, Medrano realized they weren't going to be placed back in a formation. The march was actually a walk.

"It's mind over matter," said Sergeant Washington. "Don't think about that backpack on you or your M-16. I jog every morning, and I always carry a backpack."

"Why is that, sergeant?" asked a soldier.

"I've gotten so used to the weight that now I can't jog without it. Mind over matter, soldiers."

Time went rapidly for Medrano. She did not realize how many miles she had walked nor was her body clamoring abuse. The weight did not feel like much, even with her right shoulder still bothering her on certain occasions. Her body did not seem to mind the walk. Since they were not allowed to talk, it seemed she was by herself in her thoughts of serenity.

Medrano looked at her feet which were standing over beautiful, red earth. She then turned to look at the crisp water coming down a river beside her. It was making a shushing sound. The sea-blue sky had become cloudy, and the green leaves seemed to be pointing to it.

Everything seemed shiny, as if light was projecting itself outside and inside. She could hear her heart beating with the rhythms around her.

The Great Spirit is connected to everything and everything is connected. Morningstar's words resonated in her mind.

The rain began to come down slowly. As third platoon finished, it poured down.

Saturday came fast. The sergeants told third platoon that they could go to the Cadence Club that night. Whoever wanted to stay could do so. They said the following week, seventh week, would be hectic. So they thought going to the club would be a good idea. Medrano decided to stay for numerous reasons. She had never been a partier. She liked the idea of a near-empty barracks; she wanted to straighten out her locker; and she wanted to rest before the hectic week arrived.

Females around her were busy getting ready. They were putting an extra helping of baby powder in their shirts and applying make-up. Medrano went into the latrine. When she left the stall, the only empty sink was the one next to Peck. As she walked to the sink, she had to hold a gasp. Peck was not wearing her glasses and had contact len's solution on the sink. A bottle of expensive-looking perfume was next to her, and she was in the process of expertly applying make-up. There was no fumbling on Peck's behalf as Medrano had done the first time she had applied it. The only time Medrano had seen her wear it was when they had taken the make-up class, and Peck had left on her glasses. Medrano clamped her teeth tightly over her tongue to prevent herself from saying something.

"You look so different!" exclaimed Dekan who had just walked in.

Peck looked as if she was about to say something obnoxious but then changed her mind. "Paint does that to a person."

"You should be a model, Peck," said Dekan.

Medrano remembered having told her the same thing.

"I don't think so," Peck said, finishing up and walking out of the latrine.

"Why is she made up? What got into her?" asked Dekan.

"I have no idea," Medrano answered.

Only a few females stayed. Medrano found herself contently cleaning and re-arranging her locker. Dekan walked over and sat on Medrano's bunk.

"It's a good thing you didn't go, Medrano."

"Why is that?" asked Medrano as she rolled her underwear and socks.

"Those soldiers are not going to control themselves."

"What?"

"Did you know that Rogers was making out with someone the last time we went to the Cadence Club?"

Medrano stopped rolling midway and looked at Dekan.

"You're kidding."

"Nope, she was out in the bushes somewhere. Didn't you see her hickey?" asked Dekan. "

"No. Are you B.S.'ing me, or are you on the level?"

"It's true, Medrano. Rogers met some guy at the Cadence Club and made out with him."

"Wasn't she scared to get caught?"

"Apparently not."

"I had no idea, Dekan."

"Some were even drinking that night."

"Really?"

"Yep, and you can bet your ass they'll be drinking tonight too."

Medrano finished with her locker, shined her boots, and hit the sack. She stretched vigorously in her bunk and thought how good it felt. The night before, she had been on fireguard duty. She could hardly wait to close her eyes and sleep long and hard. A couple of hours later, Dekan woke her up.

"Come with me, Medrano."

"Where?"

"Just come."

Medrano dragged herself out of bed. She followed Dekan who took her to the balcony where the fireguards were. The fireguards quickly told them to kneel down next to the half wall and not let themselves be seen.

"Why?"

"Listen, Medrano," Dekan said, giggling as quietly as she could.

"What the fuck do you mean drinking on my fucking time!" Sergeant Acosta yelled. "Now keep pushing."

"He's smoking those drunkards," said Dekan.

"This ought to teach you bunion-head drunks!" the sergeant kept screaming.

Medrano heard some vomiting sounds. "My gosh."

"Don't think I fucking feel sorry for you at all. Keep pushing!"

Medrano, Dekan, and the fireguards went back into the barracks.

"Aren't you glad you didn't go? You'd be out there being smoked even if you didn't touch a drop of liquor."

Medrano jumped back in her bunk and snuggled between the blankets. By the time the rest of third platoon had walked in, she was fast asleep. She entered the dreamworld, and she found herself in the middle of a gentle storm. The rain was pouring down, and it was washing the dirt from her fatigues and her skin. Mexican ballads by Juan Gabriel were playing, and she twirled around in the forest as the water splashed from her body.

"Med! Med!"

Was someone calling her through the rain?

"Med! Med!"

Medrano woke up and found Peck desperately calling her.

"What's wrong?" asked Medrano, jumping out of her bunk and going to Peck who was sitting up and holding her stomach.

"I'm going to be sick."

"Let's get you to the bathroom," Medrano said, getting Peck up. "Concentrate on something other than vomiting."

They quickly headed to the latrine. As soon as they reached the stall, Peck threw up. When she stopped several minutes later, she flushed the toilet.

"I feel so much better," Peck said, slurring her words.

"I hope so."

"I didn't think I was going to make it."

"I'm glad you did."

"Everything came rushing at me all of a sudden."

"That's what happens when you drink too much," said Medrano.

"Sometimes even when I don't drink, it all comes rushing at me anyway," Peck said, smiling slightly.

"I know what you mean."

"And my mind wants to explode."

"I know how you feel."

"Do you?"

"I think so."

Peck put her hands on her face and sat on the floor. "Guess who I saw a couple of days ago?"

"Who?"

"Willet."

"Really? Where?" Medrano asked.

"Sick call. She was on the bus with me."

"Did you talk to her?"

"No, and no one else did either," Peck said sadly."

That's not surprising." Peck's eyes turned glassy. "No one even sat with her. She looked lonely, like she didn't have a friend in the world."

"She probably doesn't."

"People seem to hate her."

"She's a jerk," Medrano said.

Peck put her right hand on Medrano's shoe. "Do you hate me, Med?"

"What?"

"Do you hate me?"

"Of course I don't hate you, Peck."

Peck started to cry. "My mom hated me."

"No, Peck, I'm sure she didn't," Medrano said, putting her hand on Peck's shoulder.

Her mascara was smudged. "She hated me because I let her down."

"Peck...."

"I loved my father deeply. I was his little muffin. I looked up to him." Peck put her hands on her face. "I didn't stop him. My mom must've hated me."

"How could you stop him, Peck?"

"I was 15 years old, Med, with an I.Q. of 170. I was old enough and smart enough to have done something!"

Medrano took some toilet paper and gave it to her. "Like what?"

"I should've gotten in between my mom and the gun. I tried to; but by the time I got there, my father had already shot her."

"Stop doing this to yourself, Peck. It wasn't your fault your father is an awful human being."

"I tried to save her, Med. I really did."

"You didn't pull the trigger. He did," said Medrano.

Peck calmed down after a while and asked Medrano to help her to her bunk.

"He left me alone in the world."

"You are never alone, Peck."

"It's so lonely out there, Med. Relatives didn't want to visit because I reminded them of the tragedy. Isn't that stupid?" asked Peck sadly.

"Yes, very."

"You know, Med, you're one of the nicest people I've ever met in my life."

"Thanks," said Medrano quietly.

"My mother was nice too. I loved my mother, Med," Peck whispered before she fell asleep.

"I know," whispered Medrano.

Seventh Week

Third platoon was standing outside at attention in the formation area wondering if they were going to be smoked. They could feel each other's nervous energy as they waited for one of the sergeants to say, "front-leaning-rest position." Medrano could almost feel those exhausting pushups. Sergeant Acosta paced and Sergeant Washington stood as unmovable as a rock. Get on with it, were the unspoken words hanging in the air. Medrano thought how unfair it would be if they were punished because they had lost the marching competition. But what did fairness have to do with anything?

"Third platoon," Sergeant Acosta yelled, and they braced themselves. "There was no good reason why you lost today. Do you think I was bullshitting you when I told you you were the best marchers I had ever seen? I'll tell you why you lose. You're not a team. You couldn't get it together to work as a team. And for those of you who didn't march, you were part of the team also. You could've encouraged your buddies who were marching. You could've offered to help them in any way you could."

"Nothing could've licked you as a team!" Sergeant Washington exclaimed.

"Fall in," said Sergeant Acosta. He and Sergeant Washington strode away.

Third platoon stood speechless for a couple of seconds.

"He said fall in, right?" whispered Dekan.

They finally doubletimed it to the barracks.

Medrano stood in line waiting for her turn in the pushup section of the big PT test. She thought about how no one had talked about the marching competition after the sergeants had chewed them out. But the disappointment had melted into the air molecules, making it difficult to get away from it. As the pushup line kept getting shorter, she tried concentrating on positives. "It's seventh week," she kept telling herself, "Almost done."

The soldier in front of her had completed 15 pushups and had not been able to reach the 16th before her time was up. She got off the ground with tears rolling down her face. Medrano jumped into the pushup position and started going up and down.

"One, one, one," the unfamiliar sergeant kept saying over and over. "You're not going down low enough, soldier!" he exclaimed in an annoyed fashion.

Medrano tried to go down farther so that she almost touched the ground; she finished two. Her body felt as if it weighed a thousand pounds. She could almost hear her elbows creaking. After many attempts she reached three. Then it took numerous attempts to reach four. By that time perspiration was running into her eyes, and the ground was blurred. Pain was mocking her' even tightening up her behind hurt.

"Four, four, four!" the Sergeant exclaimed.

Medrano couldn't get down far enough. All she wanted was to stand.

"That's it, soldier!" he exclaimed. He clicked his stop watch and shook his head.

Medrano did not look at him as she sprang up and headed for the situp line. No tears fell from her face—just sweat. She wiped it the best she could with her hands. The only relief she felt was that the PT tests were not judged by her own sergeants. She kept her eyes on the ground as she waited her turn.

Medrano angrily did 50 situps and did not look up at the sergeant who was smiling at her.

"That's excellent, soldier," he said, when she finished. Her head did not go up even for that.

Medrano soon found herself in the running test. When she ran once around the track, tears rushed out. She silently wiped them as she kept running. By the time she finished, she had no more tears.

"How'd you do, Medrano?" asked Morningstar as they walked into the barracks.

"I didn't pass the pushup portion of the test."

"I didn't either, but we have a couple of days before they give us another opportunity. A second test," she said as she dropped and did pushups.

"What's the use, Morningstar? If we can't do these things by now, what makes us think we can do them in a couple of days?"

Morningstar shook her head. "Speak for yourself."

"I'm just not good at the physical stuff. When am I going to learn?"

"What an easy cop out. You're running away from responsibility again. Running away from failure."

"What do you expect me to do? How am I supposed to get from 4 good pushups to 16 in a couple of days?"

"You tell me, Medrano."

"It's impossible."

"If you believe it is, then it is."

"I'll try my best and fail!"

"And so what? At worse you'll get recycled and get another shot. It's not like you'll be killed for failing."

Medrano sat on the bunk and thought about how to succeed in pulling off the enormous task of not feeling sorry for herself. She suddenly got up and dropped next to Morningstar, and started doing pushups. No words were exchanged as Morningstar smiled at her.

The next day, the sergeants announced, was for reinforcement. The final tests, called Superbowl, were around the corner. Squad leaders section off the barracks where the soldiers were to go to each section and be tested.

"You need some work on identifying your ranks, Medrano," said Rogers, who was in charge of the rank section. Medrano had messed up on some that always gave her trouble.

Medrano went to each section. She was relieved she would also have the next day to reinforce, since her memory was failing her on some of the procedures. The thing about Superbowl was that it wouldn't be a written test. It would be a "doing" test. For example, during the first-aid test, she would have to apply a dressing on a dummy. If she did it wrong, she would get a "no go." If it was perfect, then it was a "go." They had to earn a certain number of goes to pass. So far Medrano had received many "no goes" on the practice run.

That night, before turning in, she and Morningstar did some pushups. They had been dropping at every available opportunity they had. When she closed her eyes, she felt a true possibility of being able to pass. She would work extra hard the next day at reinforcing.

"Wake up, Medrano!" exclaimed the fireguard.

"What?"

"You've got KP."

Medrano shot up from bed. "You've got to be kidding."

"The sergeant left orders last night that you'd be doing KP today."

"It's not my turn."

"Deal with it," she stated.

"But I need to reinforce today."

"Tough luck."

"I just had KP last week!" Medrano exclaimed. "

"Take it up with the sergeant."

How could she take it up with the sergeants if they had not arrived. And if she did not go to KP, she would be disobeying orders. Medrano dragged herself out of her bunk, made it, and went to her locker. As she was taking off her shirt, she saw the fireguard walking around with someone behind her who was carrying a huge doll. Medrano rubbed her eyes, thinking it was a figment of her imagination. Then she heard the voice of the soldier with the doll.

"I can't go on KP," she kept saying over and over again. Medrano recognized the voice as being Dekan's.

What was Dekan doing walking around with a doll?

Medrano finished getting dressed and went to the latrine where Morningstar was entering the next stall.

"You too?" asked Medrano.

"Yes." Morningstar's voice sounded angry.

"Dekan also. The three of us went on KP last week when they woke us in the morning saying that we'd have to do KP. Those who were supposed to go were hungover from the Cadence Club the night before. They get drunk, and we got punished."

"Now we have to do it again this week instead of reinforcing!" exclaimed Medrano.

"What is with them? I know that someone has to work KP, but does it have to be us all of the time?"

"They think we are not going to pass anyway. Instead of sacrificing those who they think have a shot, they sacrifice us who they think don't."

Anger ripped through Medrano like a lightning rod.

"So we are throw-away people?" asked Medrano as her hand shook.

They arrived at KP barely on time and hardly spoke at all. They served chow, and Medrano was having a difficult time not staring into space.

Right before the day was over, Medrano went to the food-storage room and found Morningstar on the floor eating potato chips.

"Want some," Morningstar said, handing her a fresh package.

Medrano was about to say no. What if they caught them? But then she changed her mind. "Thanks," she said, grabbing the chips and sitting on the floor with her.

They munched on the chips in silence and then suddenly started laughing. The laughter turned into tears. Medrano took out tissue paper from her pocket and handed a piece to Morningstar

"This hasn't been used, has it?" asked Morningstar with a sad, mischievous smile.

Medrano laughed with pain. "Of course not."

They finished eating the chips, and Morningstar got in the pushup position. Medrano followed her lead, and they started doing pushups.

When they arrived back at the barracks, there was half-an-hour left of reinforcement. Medrano dived into her bunk.

"Aren't you going to reinforce?" asked Rogers.

"At this point, I think it's better if I get a good night's sleep. I'm tired from KP."

"But...."

"I have half-an-hour left, and all it'll serve me for is to remind me how much I don't remember."

Sleep did not take long to reach her. Her body seemed emotionally spent but calm at the same time. Her mind went deep into a dream. She was in the jungle. It was storming, and lightning was hitting from all sides. The trees were swaying so hard, it seemed to Medrano they would break in half at any moment. She swung from one edge of the jungle to another, crying desperately for it to stop storming. Suddenly, she sat in the middle of the storm with her legs in the lotus position.

"It'll be okay," Medrano kept saying over and over.

The clouds disappeared, and she was back in the desert at dawn with sprinklets of rain dancing on her skin. To her side was an eagle that looked straight at her. Then the eagle soared to the sky toward the orange rays of the sun.

"Rise and shine. Superbowl day!"

Medrano smiled as she glided from her bunk. There was nervous chatter all around her. When she was dressed, Rogers went up to her.

"Medrano," Rogers said.

"Don't tell me. KP again today," Medrano stated sarcastically.

Rogers rolled her eyes. "No. I just wanted to say good luck."

"Thanks."

Medrano went to the latrine. As she walked out of the stall, she saw Dekan patting her eyes in front of one of the mirrors.

"What's wrong?" asked Medrano, noticing Dekan's red eyes.

"Nothing."

"Are you worried about Superbowl?"

"No. It's not about stupid Superbowl." She took in a pained, chopped breath. "It's about Sammy."

"What about him?" Dekan motioned to her to go to the shower area. "I got a letter from him yesterday."

"And?"

"He dumped me. He's seeing someone else." Dekan's words were breaking.

"I'm so sorry."

"I love him so much, Medrano."

"What a jerk, doing this to you now when you're taking your final tests!" Medrano stated angrily.

"His sense of timing has always been screwed."

"No kidding."

As they went to formation, Medrano could barely contain her anger.

The sergeants finally arrived. "This is the moment of moments, third platoon. This is it soldiers. All of you have the ability to take this all the way!" exclaimed Sergeant Washington.

Sergeant Acosta nodded his head fervently. "When you're in there, act confident. Even if you don't know what you're doing, act like you do. Stay calm. Don't rush and make costly mistakes!"

"Let's go kick some ass!" Sergeant Washington exclaimed.

On the way to the testing range, they sang Medrano's favorite cadence:

Standing tall and looking good now,

your left wo-oh your left now

Ought to be in Hollywood now

your left wo-oh your left now

When they arrived at the range, Medrano looked around at all the females from the different platoons. She wondered who would make it, and who would fail. By the end of the day, for better or worse, it would at least be somewhat over, even if she had to be recycled.

"You'll be fine, Med." Peck broke into her thoughts.

Medrano smiled at her. "You too, not only here but in everything."

"Thanks."

The soldiers wished each other luck. Somewhere inside of me, Medrano thought, I know all this stuff. The individual squads went first. The range was divided in sections for each test. The first section would be the code of conduct when a sergeant appeared. There were benches in a circle, and Medrano sat on one with Rogers while others sat on the other benches. A sergeant suddenly sliced by them, walking extremely fast. By the time Medrano and Rogers shot up, followed procedure, and said, "Good morning, sergeant," he had left. The others on the remaining benches managed to do it on time.

Medrano and Rogers took the cards with "goes" and "no goes" for each section of the test to a sergeant. He was sitting in front of the section watching everything. On each of their cards, he clipped off a "no go" with a hand clipper.

As they waited in line for the next section, Roger's mouth was trembling.

"Shit! That was the easiest one. How did we mess it up, Medrano?"

"The sergeant came out of nowhere. The others were able to see him on time because he walked past us first."

"Shit!"

The next test was more in Medrano's territory. They walked into a room and took a multiple-choice, written test. They identified the different kinds of terrain features. Medrano finished before anyone else did, and the sergeant rewarded her with a "go."

"Shit!" Rogers said when she walked out. "I got two wrong, so I got a "no go." I knew the right answer, but I second guessed myself. Shit!"

The next test was marching. The sergeant there gave Medrano a "no go" because she had not been aligned properly. She told herself not to panic. Everything would be okay regardless of how it turned out that day. Rogers was jumping for joy because she had gotten a "go."

The next test was saluting an officer indoors and also telling rank. Medrano prayed she would be able to remember.

The test started outside. Medrano walked into the room. When she got to the officers' desk, she stopped, stood at attention, and saluted.

"Sir, Private Medrano reporting for duty," she said.

The officer saluted her back. As she lowered her hand, he said,

"At ease, soldier."

Medrano stood in parade rest, and the officer took out some cards with pictures of ranks. "What's this rank, soldier?"

"Sir, that is a Specialist...."

Shoot, she thought as she stared at the upside-down triangle which was round at the top with two stripes and a bird in the middle. There were several different kinds of specialists, and all that made them different was the stripes on top of the upside-down triangle. What were the numbers? Was it a Specialist Six, Five or Four?

The officer waited for her answer. As Medrano was about to blurt out an answer, she remembered what Sergeant Acosta had said, "Be calm." Inside herself she heard a shout say Specialist Six. First instincts were good instincts thought Medrano.

"Sir, that is a Specialist Six."

"Very good, soldier."

When the "go" was clipped on her card, she almost danced.

I can't believe I messed it up!" Rogers exclaimed. "It was a Specialist, and I guessed a Specialist Six."

Sergeant Acosta shook his head. "I know you know this shit, Rogers. You're trying too hard. That's why you're screwing up."

"The more you get 'no goes,' the more you blind yourself of the possibility of getting 'goes.' Then you keep the bad momentum going," said Sergeant Washington.

Medrano went on to do the rest of the tests in areas such as first aid, code-of-conduct toward officers outside, decontamination of self in case of chemical warfare, firing the M-16 and other weapons, etc. She was earning "goes" and "no goes." But the main thing was that she was having fun, unlike several other females like Rogers who were walking around glassy-eyed.

When she finished the tests, the names of those who had passed were called. Peck had made it, but Medrano's name was not called. Nor was Dekan's.

"There are some of you who almost made it but didn't quite get there. We're going to allow you to go back and try to change some 'no goes' into 'goes,'" an officer stated.

Medrano held her breath.

"Medrano," the officer said, "today is your lucky day. You're right in the middle with eight "no goes." One more and you would have not been given this chance. We're letting you go back, soldier."

She was told she needed to get four more "goes" and in order to pass. The sergeant finished calling the names of those who would be allowed to go back. Rogers sobbed when her name was not called. Medrano never thought a person like Rogers cried.

"Those of you who didn't pass will get another shot at this in a week."

"At least we won't automatically be recycled," said Dekan.

"One more week in this hellhole," answered Rogers.

Medrano went back to the first test. Again, the sergeant came out of nowhere. She got a "no go." I can't believe this, she thought. But she stopped herself from panicking by chuckling. It's okay. I can handle this.

As she walked to the next range, her mind resonated with positive words. Then she earned three consecutive "goes." One more, she thought. Unfortunately, the next one was a "no go." Her head started hurting, and her mind raced. What if I fail? I'm so close to succeeding.

What if?

What if?

What if?

Medrano closed her eyes and remembered the storm in her dream. She sat down. In her mind she said, "What if I fail? So what?" The storm left, and the desert blossomed. She faced the eagle and kept saying, "So what!" The eagle responded through its mind into Medrano's, the 'so what' is the journey. It extended its huge, brown wings. As it soared, Medrano smiled and extended her hand to touch the orange glints of the dawn. Medrano opened her eyes and walked to her next test.

"Congratulations, soldier, you passed," said the sergeant after the test. He punched a "go" on her card.

Medrano thumped her head to make sure she was not day-dreaming. She doubletimed it back to her platoon who were waiting for those who were repeating the tests.

"How'd you do, Medrano?" asked Sergeant Acosta, not looking very confident.

"I passed."

"You did?"

Medrano lifted her chin. "Yes, sergeant."

"Very good, soldier."

"What can I say, sergeant. I'm good."

Sergeant Acosta laughed. The other soldiers went up to her and patted her on the back. Medrano was thrilled to hear Canela and García had also passed.

"Congrats," said Dekan.

"I'm sorry about...."

"Hey, I've got another shot at this in a week. I'm okay."

"Are you really okay?" asked Medrano.

"Yes."

"You're very brave," Medrano stated.

"I'm so happy for you," said Morningstar walking up to Medrano.

"How'd you do?"

"Go."

"Great."

"Can you believe I passed on the first try?"

Medrano chuckled. "I can believe that."

"We didn't need that second day of reinforcement after all."

"That'll teach them to throw us away," whispered Medrano as she looked at the sergeants in the distance.

"You bet."

The next day Medrano found herself re-taking the PT test. Morningstar had taken it before her and had passed. As she was on the ground doing pushups, Medrano thought about the eagle in her dream instead of thinking about the weight of her body or the pain in her elbows.

"One, two, three," said the sergeant, "four, five, six, seven, eight." Medrano looked into the eagle's eyes.

"Seven, eight, nine."

She wanted to stop so badly. If she did, would she be able to go on?

"Ten, eleven, twelve, thirteen."

"Don't give in now!"

"Thirteen, fourteen."

Two more. No pain, no gain, she said to herself.

"Fifteen, sixteen, seventeen, eighteen!"

Medrano dropped to the ground.

"You made it, soldier!"

Medrano smiled as she sprang from the ground. The situps and the running test became a blur to her. Her heart beat kept saying, "I made it! I made it!" The euphoria of it was the only thing she wanted to experience.

When she ran into the barracks, she exclaimed, "I'm out of here! No more basic training!" Medrano received a round of hugs.

Following graduation, the graduates of basic training would be leaving for AIT, advanced individual training. They were in the barracks packing. As Medrano went to the latrine, she noticed García was sitting in front of her locker. Her possessions were spread all around her in a chaotic mess, and she stared into space.

"What's wrong, García?"

"I can't do this."

"Do what?" asked Medrano.

"Pack."

"Why not?"

"I got too much stuff. How am I going to get all this stuff in my duffel bag?"

Medrano chuckled. "I'm sure you'll find a way."

Medrano went to the latrine and thought of not caring about getting everything in her duffel bag—as long as she was able to leave basic. If necessary, she would throw away her deodorant and personals as long as she could have some freedom. When she walked back to her bunk, she started stuffing everything into her duffel bag, not bothering to fold or neatly pack.

"In a hurry, aren't you?" asked Peck.

"You bet."

The only things she left out were her uniform, shoes, and shoe shining kit. She noticed a group around Canela's bunk shining their shoes. She promptly grabbed her stuff, and plopped herself next to García.

"Found a way to pack?" Medrano asked.

García frowned. "I don't know how I acquired that much stuff in this place."

As Medrano started shining her shoes, Morningstar grabbed the shoes from her.

"What are you doing?" asked Medrano.

"I owe you, remember?"

"Actually, I think I owe you," Medrano said, trying to grab them back. Morningstar would not let them go.

"We had a deal," she said, starting to shine them. "I'm so happy to be shining these to get out of here even though I'm staying at Fort Jackson for AIT."

"I'm leaving for Fort Benning, Georgia," said García.

"I'm staying here too," Medrano said. "My MOS is 71 Lima."

"Administrative Specialist?" asked Canela.

"Yep."

"Me too," Canela said.

"As soon as I pass Superbowl next week, I'll be heading for Fort Sam Houston in San Antonio to be a medic," said Dekan.

Peck quietly sat down with her kit next to Medrano.

"Where are you going, Peck?"

"Here. I'm a 71 Lima."

"I just can't believe this is almost over. We're graduating!" exclaimed García with a flushed face.

"What does it all mean?" asked Canela as she stood.

"What?" asked Medrano.

"What's the purpose of being happy? The world is all screwed up with wars, racism, sexism, diseases, rapes, mutilations, child abuse, wife beating, sexual harassment, and so on! What's the use? What's the purpose?"

Silence filled the area as smiles left faces and contemplative looks replaced them.

"We're the purpose," said Medrano almost in a whisper.

"What?" asked Canela.

"Our dreams, ambitions, loves, spirituality—that's the purpose," Medrano said confidently.

"But what if someone takes them from us? Robs them?" asked Dekan.

Medrano smiled. "Remember what Sergeant Acosta said? Together nothing can lick us."

Morningstar nodded her head. "Especially if we stay together in here," she said, pointing at her heart.

Remember that your safety net is yourself, Adela," said Medrano.

Peck opened her mouth. "Maybe...." Everyone stared at her with narrowed eyes.

"Yes?" asked Medrano.

"Maybe that's true," Peck finished saying.

As third platoon marched to graduation, Medrano couldn't help thinking this would be the last time they marched together, such as when she took her last PT test. Everything was becoming a blur, as if it was happening simultaneously—fast and in slow motion

Once inside the building, Medrano took note of the stage. It had a white banner over the edge with the words "All the Way" written in a gray and red outline. The hats belonging to the drill sergeants and officers were on the front edge of the stage.

One by one, third platoon went on the stage where the officers and sergeants stood at attention. They saluted the officers and shook hands with them and the sergeants. Then they received their diplomas.

This year Medrano had gone through two graduations. This one was definitely the shorter but more intense one.

Vignettes of basic came quickly to Medrano. She saw all the disappointments and failures clearly. How had she reached this point? In the beginning it seemed impossible to envision herself graduating. How did she, the PT flunkee, get here? She wondered how everyone else felt. Did they feel they were simultaneously leaving something behind as they entered another world? That world outside of basic training.

As the ceremony ended, Medrano kept telling herself the graduation was really happening. She had graduated from high school, joined the military, and for all intents and purposes was out of basic training. It was not a movie.

Once outside she kept hugging soldiers. Some parents and husbands were able to make it to graduation, and Medrano was introduced to them.

"Medrano, this is my husband," said Walker.

Medrano shook hands with a handsome man in a blue suit.

"Pleased to meet you."

"Likewise," he said.

"The sergeants didn't think Medrano would make it through; but at the last moment, she pulled out the lead. knew she would," Walker stated smiling.

Medrano grinned. "Thanks."

The majority of the soldiers were like Medrano and had families too far away to attend. However, it did not dim the smiles. As Medrano and some of the other females went back to the barracks which were full of soldiers coming in and out, tears came to Medrano's eyes. In the high school ceremony, she had seen many of her peers crying. She had not been able to muster one tear. She had said, "Good riddance. I'm glad I'm out of here."

"I ship now," said García sadly.

Medrano, Peck, Morningstar, and Dekan helped her with her gear. They walked outside where dozens of soldiers were standing around or sitting on their duffel bags freely talking away.

"That must be my ride," said García, pointing at a carting truck.

"You've got my new address with you?" asked Medrano.

"Yes, do you have mine?"

"Of course."

"Write to us!" exclaimed Canela as she hugged her.

"You too." García said.

They hugged her one-by-one as tears flowed. They stared at her as she got on the truck. No one talked until the truck left.

"This is really happening," said Medrano. Everyone nodded their head.

They said good-bye to some of the other third platoon soldiers who were shipping out.

"We don't ship out for another hour," said Peck, "Let's go eat one last time at the mess-hall."

Peck, Medrano, Morningstar, and Dekan walked to the mess-hall. Medrano could not shake the feeling of all this being abnormal. Shouldn't she be doubletiming it? They waited in a line outside the mess-hall without having to be in formation first or standing at attention. Everyone chattered, and Medrano realized it was the first time she had heard so much noise in the mess-hall. They picked up their food and sat down to eat.

"One more hour, and we'll be through," sang Medrano in a whisper.

Peck chuckled. "Speak up. We don't have to whisper anymore."

They ate the rest of their chow in silence, and Medrano kept looking around with an uncomfortable feeling. When they finished, they went back to the barracks. The barracks had an eerie feeling of completion—of silence. It was not the same kind of silence that Medrano had experienced while pulling fireguard duty at night. It was solitary silence, as if the barracks knew they were about to be abandoned.

Except for Dekan, Medrano and the grabbed their gear and were about to walk out the double doors when they took one last look.

"It's not going to be the same being here without all of you," said Dekan, "It'll be one hell of a long week."

Everyone nodded sadly.

"Let's do it. Let's go all the way," said Canela. She walked out without glancing back even once. Everyone followed her.

They went to the section where other soldiers from third platoon were waiting.

"Third platoon!" Sergeant Acosta exclaimed. He and Sergeant Washington walked toward them.

They shot up.

"At ease," said Sergeant Washington.

"I want those of you staying at Fort Jackson to promise us you'll come back and visit," announced Sergeant Acosta.

There was a stunned silence.

"You'll be getting passes from AIT, and I hope you come and say hello to your old drill sergeants."

"Yes, sergeant," said Canela smiling. "We'll come back and visit."

"Good luck," both sergeants said as they left.

After they left everyone started talking at the same time. Medrano stared after them. They were passing the soda and ice cream machines, the same ones from which they had never been allowed to buy.

"I'll be right back," said Medrano as she started doubletiming it. "I really need to do something."

When she arrived at the machines, she quickly took out coins and jammed them into the slots. She picked out a Coke and a chocolate-covered ice cream bar with nuts.

"How is it?" asked Peck who had walked up behind her and was putting coins into the machine.

"It's the best Coke and ice cream I've ever had."

"We just had soda and ice cream in the mess-hall."

Medrano smiled. "I know."

Peck took a gulp from her root beer soda. "You're right about this being the best, though, Eliza."

Medrano raised an eyebrow. "What's your first name, anyway, Peck?"

"Violet."

"Violet?!"

"You don't think it suits me?"

"No, not really."

Peck laughed. "Neither do I."

"How's the ice cream?"

Peck took a bite from her sandwich ice cream. "Life can pretty much suck eggs, but sometimes it can be fucking good."

"Sometimes?"

They walked back to Canela. She cast an understanding grin at Medrano who was still eating her ice cream.

"I hope AIT doesn't suck," said Peck.

They started discussing AIT. Medrano grinned warmly as her eyes darted around the room. The voices grew fainter as the soldiers walked farther and father away. The eagle's eyes flashed in front of her.

She slowly looked at each soldier. Each seemed as familiar as her favorite books—each a different story, a different journey. Morningstar smiled at her. This mindreading business was really something. At a distance, she could hear soldiers singing cadence:

Standing tall and looking good now,

your left wo-oh your left now

Ought to be in Hollywood now

Your left wo-oh your left now